A
CANDLELIGHT REGENCY SPECIAL

D0774525

CANDLELIGHT REGENCIES

THE
FAINT-HEARTED
FELON

Pauline Pryor

A CANDLELIGHT REGENCY SPECIAL

Published by
Dell Publishing Co., Inc.
1 Dag Hammarskjold Plaza
New York, New York 10017

Dell ® TM 681510, Dell Publishing Co., Inc.

ISBN: 0-440-12506-5

Printed in the United States of America
First printing—July 1981

THE FAINT-HEARTED FELON

CHAPTER ONE

"Poor Papa," Imogene declared, stabbing away at her embroidery with more energy than skill, "I declare that being a justice of the peace puts him in a dreadful temper. Only listen to the way he is shouting at poor Randolph. I wonder you allow him to go on that way, Mama. Indeed I do. I'm certain that Alicia must be quite put out of countenance by the racket he is making."

Alicia avoided her cousin's eyes and let her fingers wander lightly up and down the keys of the pianoforte. As a guest in Sir Humphrey's household, she thought it politic not to criticize him, even though it was quite true that he was creating a clamor in the library. Alicia had only been in Bath for two weeks, but that had been ample time for her to gather that her uncle's temper was uncertain at best. She dreaded to think what a dreadful countenance he must turn on the unfortunate miscreants who came before the bar where he was justice of the peace.

"Why, what can I do to stop him?" Lady Fairbreaks declared in an agitated manner. She was a generously proportioned woman of a certain age who sought to hide both of those factors by the adroit use of a tightly laced corset and the application of vermillion to her cheeks with such a lavish hand that she usually appeared to be burning up with fever. In all other respects, however, she was elegance itself with her powdered hair raised in the new style to about a foot in front, and a pink silk gown with an extraordinarily low-cut décolletage.

"Dear Mama," Imogene said impatiently. "You know that if you like you can twist Papa around your little finger."

"What a curious way of expressing it," Lady Fairbreaks mused. "But you are quite mistaken, you know. When your father is in one of his fits, I declare he terrifies me."

Imogene laughed, and even Alicia could not suppress a smile. Only yesterday, when the tradesmen had brought the bills her aunt had run up during the last quarter, she had seen her uncle rage about this very room like a mad bull while her aunt played with the kitten and hummed a little song under her breath for all the world as though she did not hear him.

"The only reason you do not intervene in my brother's behalf at this very moment, Mama," Imogene went on, casting her embroidery aside, "is because you do not care to make the effort. Come. Confess it."

"Fatigued would be a better word, my pet," Lady Fairbreaks said with a vague smile. "There was such a dreadful crush at the Assembly Room last night that I have had a megrim all of today. Besides, Randolph has been such a naughty fellow! I declare he quite deserves to be called down."

Lady Fairbreaks was pacing the room in her usual restless way as she talked, and now Imogene rose and joined her. Mother and daughter made a quaint contrast, the one refurbished like an overhauled carriage and the other sober as a sparrow in her neat blue gown, with a white neckerchief modestly draped around her neck and shoulders and her fair curls pulled into a knot at the back of her well-shaped head.

"The poor child will never find a husband," Lady Fairbreaks had confided to Alicia several times during the past two weeks. "I declare she drives me to distraction. It seems a bit unfair that I should have to be the one to lure unsuspecting young gentlemen to this house. But there it is! Imogene never has been enterprising. And, of course, although she is not unattractive, she is not a natural beauty."

At that point she always preened herself with such little regard for modesty that Alicia was hard put not to smile. It had not taken her long to discover that her aunt was awash with vanity and that nothing pleased her more than to have it thought that she attracted her daughter's suitors for her. Indeed, there had been a few unpleasant moments when Alicia had first arrived on her visit and was observed by Lady Fairbreaks to have

11

"quite grown up," a state of affairs which had not seemed to fill her aunt with delight.

"My dear niece," she had said, looking Alicia up and down, "I never dreamed that you would grow into such a beauty. Indeed I cannot think where you get your looks, for it is a well-known fact that your poor mama could never hold a candle to me. La, everyone would say so, even though I begged them not to! Still, red hair like yours is not quite the fashion, I think, and now that I look closely I see your nose is inclined to tilt."

Within a few minutes, by virtue of depreciating each of Alicia's features in turn, Lady Fairbreaks had managed to work her way into a good humor again and was quite content to introduce her niece to everyone as "Poor Ruth's daughter." "But then," she would add, "I'm sure that if you could see my sister you would note the resemblance this child here bears to her." All of which did not trouble Alicia in the slightest although, when they were alone together, Imogene raged about it.

"Mama *will* make herself impossible," she confided. "Unless she can convince herself that no one can hold a candle to her, she is quite miserable. I have tried and tried, but I can do nothing with her."

But now it appeared that Imogene was prepared to make one more attempt to deal with her mother.

"You must tell me what Randolph has been

about this time," she demanded, taking Lady Fairbreaks's arm and compelling her to stop her posturing. "Come. You must tell me!"

"La, my dear, do not tug me about so," her mother declared. "Is it my fault that you will not see your brother as the rake he is?"

"A rake, Mama! Surely you exaggerate in order to annoy me. He is no more fond of cards than any other young gentleman of style, I think, and if he will take a glass or two of claret too many from time to time, what is out of the ordinary about that?"

Alicia had become familiar with Imogene's constant defense of her brother, and she admired her for it even though, having observed her cousin Randolph with a clearer eye, she had a strong suspicion that his mother's evaluation of his character was closer to being accurate. At the very least it was fair enough to say that Randolph was singularly easy in his ways and that Sir Humphrey might well be making an accurate prediction when he declared, as he was fond of doing, that one of these days his own son would be making an appearance before him in his official capacity as justice of the peace.

"Life must be taken more seriously than that, sir," he would declare whenever one of Randolph's misadventures would come to his attention. "Life must be taken very seriously indeed, as I am convinced you will learn to your discomfort."

All of which advice Randolph would accept

with the greatest good humor and promise to reform in a way which deceived no one.

"But what has he *done*, Mama?" Imogene persisted now. "If it is that little matter of an altercation between him and the Marquess of Sheldon, I declare that I do not blame Randolph for refusing to put up with his insulting ways."

"It is a far more grave offense than that, my dear," Lady Fairbreaks assured her. "And if you are not as shocked by it as I am, I am certain that your cousin will see the seriousness of it straight away."

Alicia inclined her head in such a way as to indicate neither one thing nor the other, having determined early on not to take sides in this inflammatory household.

"Alicia cannot be suitably shocked until you tell us what Randolph has done, Mama," Imogene declared. "There is no use trying to keep it a secret, you know. All that I need to do is to go to the door of the library and listen for a minute and I will soon know all about it."

"Your father does not condone eavesdropping," Lady Fairbreaks said stiffly.

"If all judges are like Papa, they are too judgmental by far," Imogene observed with what Alicia thought uncommon boldness. It was, she thought, very strange that in a household where so much was said about right and wrong and good behavior, the son should be a scamp and the daughter a scold.

"I will not have a word said against your father," Lady Fairbreaks observed, wielding her fan with a will. "He is completely justified in being beside himself with rage. Only fancy! Your brother has dared to criticize him! Will you believe that the young cub has challenged one of the decisions which Papa made this morning when he was serving as justice?"

She had promised to shock Alicia and, indeed, she had succeeded. Sir Humphrey was not the sort of man one challenged in or out of his own courtroom.

"You must be mistaken, Mama," Imogene declared, going quite pale. "Randolph would never go to court unless he had to. You know his opinion of the law in general."

"It is like your brother to carp and carry on about things he knows nothing of," Lady Fairbreaks announced. "I am not interested in his opinion of the law. I am only relieved that he has not yet broken it."

"Randolph would never do that," Imogene cried, easily diverted into defending her brother on another score. "He may not respect the law, but he has a considerable regard for the penalties it accords."

She did not add that Randolph did not count bravery as one of the major virtues, but Alicia, who had seen her cousin blanch at the mere description of a duel, thought that might be taken into consideration, as well.

"That's as may be, miss," Lady Fairbreaks announced tartly. "Your father likes to say your brother will hang one day."

That being the remark that was saved for moments when her aunt wanted to drive her daughter into a near frenzy, Alicia thought it time to interpose.

"And why was my cousin in court, Aunt?" she said, rising from the pianoforte seat, a slim figure in a green and white striped muslin gown with her thick mass of red curls tumbled half in, half out of her white mobcap.

"Did I not say you would be shocked, Alicia?" Lady Fairbreaks announced triumphantly.

"Indeed you did, ma'am. But I am curious, as well."

"Yes. Very natural that you should be. Well, I shall tell all if you both insist."

Lady Fairbreaks was very fond of giving in whenever she decided to, meanwhile claiming to have been forced into it in spite of her better judgment. It was one of her many small pretenses, like that of being terrified of her husband when he was in a fury or the fiction that the house teemed with young men whom she had lured there for Imogene's sake.

Now she took command of the room with a dramatic intensity which would have done a Siddons proud. One expected a round of applause. "Randolph," Lady Fairbreaks announced. "Your brother, Imogene! Your cousin, Alicia!"

"And your son, Mama," Imogene groaned, sinking onto a chair in mock exhaustion. "Cannot

16

you get to the point without making such a spin-about affair of it? Why was Randolph in court in the first place?"

"Young Soupcon. Lord Soupcon's youngest son."

"Do make sense, Mama."

"I am about to, miss. You wanted me to make quick work of it and I am doing so. Randolph was there because his fine friend Soupcon was arrested by one of the watchmen last night."

Alicia saw Imogene's face fall and knew the reason. Certain as it was that Randolph would never break the law himself, he had many more friends who did so in a minor way than quite pleased his sister.

"Don't you want to know the charge, my dear?" Lady Fairbreaks demanded archly. "I know that you will make some excuse for him. Say he was in his cups. As, no doubt, he was. But the charge is breaking the king's peace, and that is a different matter."

"But Randolph? Was he a witness?"

Lady Fairbreaks raised her chin in such a manner as to reduce the number of her chins by one. "He *claims* to be," she said. "He *claims* a good many things, including the fact that it is his *opinion* that your father has ruled wrongly in finding young Soupcon guilty of assault."

There was a moment of suspenseful silence as Lady Fairbreaks took a stroll around the room, admiring herself in the mirrors which adorned each of the four walls and humming a little song, which was only one of what Sir Humphrey succinctly called his wife's "maddening habits."

"Well," Imogene said at last. "Go on, Mama. Tell us the rest of it."

Lady Fairbreaks completed her progress by wandering in the direction of the door. "As for the rest," she said, "you must ask your father, Imogene. Ah, here he is now! What can Randolph be about, my dear, slamming out of the house that way? No, no. Don't tell me. I have a frightful megrim and must go and lie down for a while. Remember that I have my looks to think of. Trot along and talk to the girls, dear. I believe they have some questions to ask you, although I can't imagine what about."

CHAPTER TWO

Sir Humphrey was not a tall man, but there was a certain massive quality about his construction which made it appear that he filled any room he entered. His brown wig with its sausage-roll curls on either side was a fitting frame for his broad face, which was marred by nothing more out of the ordinary than a slightly scarlet, bulbous nose. His costume was quite as commonplace as his face except that the skirts of his coat challenged fashion by extending below his knees, and his embroidered waistcoat seemed to have been cut for a larger man, as well. It was, Alicia thought, as though his tailor had been deceived by Sir Humphrey's pomposity into thinking he was fitting someone a size larger than he really was.

"What's all this then?" her uncle announced as he burst into the sitting room. "What sort of questions, eh? I'm in no mood for nonsense, mind."

It was not absolutely necessary, Alicia thought, for him to inform them of that particular fact. Indeed, the twist of her uncle's mouth, the glint

19

of his eyes, and the apoplectic state of his complexion made it rather more than simply apparent that if one wanted to talk nonsense, one should go somewhere else.

"I shouldn't call it nonsense to want to know why you were giving Randolph such a calling down, I'm sure," Imogene said tartly.

Alicia never failed to be taken by surprise by the impertinence with which her cousin treated both her parents. Even more amazing was the fact that, although Lady Fairbreaks responded by playing her little games and Sir Humphrey shouted, neither of them ever took steps to see that their daughter curbed her tongue in future. In fact, Alicia had the strange feeling that under all the fuss and bluster both Sir Humphrey and his wife were a little afraid of their children. Certainly it was a strange family life they lived, one which did not remind her in the slightest of her quiet home in a Sussex vicarage, where her father spent every spare hour puttering in the garden and her mother bustled happily around the kitchen.

"You'll find life at Bath quite a different experience, my dear," her father had told Alicia when she had received the invitation two months ago. "This is very generous of your aunt and uncle, for they know we cannot afford a coming out for you in London."

And, because it had been a considerable time since Mrs. Eaton had seen her sister, it was decided that when Alicia's visit came to an end, she would travel to Bath to fetch her.

"The last time your aunt and uncle came to visit us, you were just a child," Mrs. Eaton had said wistfully. "I always wondered if dear Frances were't just a little ashamed of us."

And then, fearful that she might have hurt her husband's feelings, she had kissed him fondly and declared that she had only meant to make the point that they did not live in the grand manner that she supposed her sister was accustomed to in Bath.

"Balls nearly every night, I believe," she said. "Your aunt will be able to introduce you to the crème de la crème. At least that is how she refers to her friends in her letters, although I never have been certain precisely what that meant. But I am certain it will all be quite exciting, what with your cousins being almost just your age."

And then she had hurried off to deal with some crisis in the kitchen in response to sounds of dismay coming from the little maid who was their only servant, and Alicia had been left alone with her father, to whom she had confided that she did not like to go to visit anyone who might condescend.

"If they are too good to come here, as Mama says," she had said with a toss of her head, "then I am too good to go there, I fancy."

The vicar had laughed at that. He was a good-natured, rotund little man who was better known for the excellence of his temper than the quality of his sermons.

"Your aunt and uncle have faults just as any one of us, my dear," he said, "but condescension is not one of them. They are too busy with their own affairs to bother to come to see us, that is all. And it has always been too great an expense for us to go all the way to Bath."

And when Alicia had protested that there was the cost of sending her there to consider, her father had announced the existence of a little nest egg set aside for just such a purpose.

"It will please your mother to have you see something of society," he said. "You have a strong character, my dear, and I trust you to make your own decisions as to what to like and dislike about the world. But clearly you should see something more than this small corner of Sussex."

Alicia had been relieved that nothing had been said about the need for her to make a good match. Neither of her parents was ambitious in that quarter, caring only to see her happy. But no doubt they thought it only right that they should give her every advantage, and with that in mind Alicia had embarked on her visit determined to enjoy herself.

As it happened, that had been easy enough to do. Her aunt and uncle might have their peculiar ways, but they were kind people at heart and made Alicia feel at home by the simple expedient of accepting her as one of the family, with no formalities. If Lady Fairbreaks was vain and Sir Humphrey bombastic, that was simply their way. As for Imogene and Randolph, Alicia had taken to both of them from the start. And certainly there was excitement enough, what with a constant round of entertainment, starting with their trip to take the waters at the Pump Room every morning, not to mention the Assembly Room dancing at night, where, between fops fresh down from London and grand ladies with their extravagant ways, Alicia's interest was never given a chance to flag.

"And what makes you think I *was* giving your brother a calling down, miss?" Sir Humphrey demanded now.

"I am not deaf, Papa," Imogene retorted. "You could be heard throughout the house and, I have no doubt, up and down the street as well. Why, sir, I do not dare to look out the window for fear of seeing that a crowd has collected to listen to you."

"By gad, girl! That is no way for a gel to address her father!"

Sir Humphrey pursed his lips and filled his ruddy cheeks with air, giving the impression that he might be about to explode. When Alicia had first witnessed such an attack, she had been afraid that her uncle would bring on apoplexy, but by now she knew that far from being in a passion, he was only showing what was, for him, mild displeasure.

"It's just that I don't think you're fair to Randolph," Imogene replied. "After all, he is a grown man, and if he wants to offer up a criticism or two . . ."

"A what!"

"A criticism. Mama said that . . ."

"Damme!" Sir Humphrey roared, "is a man to have no privacy in this house? Is a man never to be let alone and not be troubled by meddling women? Is a man never to be treated with the respect he deserves? It makes my bile rise, indeed it does! It makes my fly into the boughs!"

Alicia decided that the time had come for her to leave the room as quietly and unobtrusively as she was able. She had never seen her uncle this distressed before, and she did not care for the defiant gleam in Imogene's eyes. A major explosion seemed to be in the making, and she did not want to be in the vicinity when it occurred.

But she had no sooner gathered her skirts around preparatory to taking flight than her uncle turned his full attention on her.

"Do not think that I include you in these remarks, my dear," he said, clearly struggling to gain control of himself. "Now then, a judge has need of a jury and I have need of you."

"Would you not prefer to be private with your daughter, sir?" Alicia said hopefully. "I thought I might just run up to my room and . . ."

Her uncle interrupted her before she had come to some conclusion about what she would run up the stairs to do.

"I confess to having very little desire to be private with any immediate member of my family just at present," Sir Humphrey said. "But since, apparently, I must at least communicate with them, I would like a detached opinion of the way in which I proceed. I am a man inclined to too much heat on occasion. Or so I have been told. It is only that the follies of the world are enough to drive a sane and sensible man like myself mad, I assure you. And then, of course, there are the grave responsibilities which a justice of the peace must bear."

Alicia realized that before her stood a man with an ego so sensitive that it could not bear the slightest scratch to its delicate surface. And yet Randolph had been chipping away at that same surface with a will, and thus, to complete the metaphor, before her stood a cracked cup which needed mending.

"Everyone appreciates that, Uncle," she said warmly. "Why, since I have come to Bath I have met no one who speaks of you other than with the greatest respect."

That, of course, was not strictly true, since among the people she had talked to were Imogene and Randolph, but Alicia thought that the occasion called for a small lie at the very least. And then, because she was being rewarded by one of her uncle's rare smiles, she could not resist plunging ahead.

"And, large as this city is, I have not met a single person who does not know of you, sir," she assured him. "Your reputation is of the sort which is not easily established, Uncle. You should be congratulated on it."

Alicia kept her eyes fixed on her uncle's face as she spoke, aware that Imogene, was was standing turned away from him, was trying on expressions of incredulity as one might try on masks.

"Quite so, my dear! Quite so!" Sir Humphrey replied, his spirits quickly revived. "And yet, in spite of this, would you believe that my own son has dared to criticize me?"

This question placed Alicia in an awkward position, which Imogene's grin indicated that she richly deserved as a reward for having been so fulsome in her flattery.

"I am very sorry to hear it, sir," Alicia murmured.

"Well said, gel! Well said! And because I have your sympathy and understanding, I want you to hear the exact ins and outs of it. I intend to tell the story to *you* and not to some other person who might happen to be in this room, you understand."

Alicia mustered up a faint smile, hoping that it would relieve her of the necessity of making any other response.

"Well then," Sir Humphrey continued, plunking himself down in a wing chair and crossing his white-stockinged legs. "The facts are these, my dear niece. This morning one of the watchmen, old Pilchorn, brought a certain young gentleman by the name of Jonathan Soupcon, Esquire, before the bar on a charge of assault and battery.

Old Pilchorn said the fellow had broken his stick and done a mischief to his lantern. Now, what do you think of that?"

"I think I'd need to know what Mr. Soupcon had to say for himself before I voiced an opinion," Imogene said. "I hope you troubled yourself to ask for the other side of the story, Papa."

"Do I hear a fly buzzing somewhere in the room?" Sir Humphrey demanded, addressing himself to Alicia. "What do *you* think, my dear?"

Alicia thought it the better part of wisdom to answer one question with another. "Is Mr. Pilchorn very old?" she said demurely. "I only mean it seems like a very odd job for an old man."

"Pilchorn?" Sir Humphrey replied, diverted. "Well now, he must be getting on to seventy. There's not much that fellow hasn't seen, I can tell you. Knows all there is to know about Bath after night, hey!"

"Well, if the man is only seventy, he's a mere boy when compared to the other watchmen the town employs," Imogene observed. "The older they are, the cheaper they come, and if they are halt and blind as well, all the better."

Sir Humphrey cleared his throat, making no indication that anyone had spoken by as much as a turn of his head. "Now," he said, "when I challenged Mr. Soupcon accordingly, I observed a certain shiftiness about the eyes which set me on my guard. And, of course, since he is a young man, it had to be assumed that he was in his cups the night before. You follow me, my dear? There are certain subtleties about the working of the legal mind which you may find confusing."

Behind her father's chair, Imogene made a great, silent show of falling into a great fit of laughter. Accordingly, Alicia concentrated all her efforts on keeping her eyes trained to her uncle's face.

"Yes, sir," she said. "That is quite clear to me, I think."

"*Some* people might find it difficult to comprehend," Sir Humphrey said, "that a man of my years of training and my innate fineness of judgment might be able to reach a decision before all the evidence is in. But that is the way of it, I assure you. And in this case it was quite clear to me that the defendant was guilty."

Finding that she could not go so far as to commend him, Alicia tried another question.

"And did you say so, Uncle, there and then?" she asked with all the innocence she could muster.

"Damme, I voiced a few opinions about the scandalous behavior of young gentlemen today," Sir Humphrey replied. "A lecture is as good as a sentence with some of these young coxcombs, I've discovered. If only their fathers were to give them some sound advice . . ."

"The sort of advice you give Randolph, Papa?" Imogene said in a low voice.

"Precisely the same kind of advice, miss!" Sir Humphrey shouted, forgetting for the moment that his daughter was not to be acknowledged to be in the room. "It is not my fault that the young gudgeon will not take it!"

The color rose and fell in his face again, and he gave two mighty puffs, slapped the palms of his hands on the arms of the chair, and regained control of himself.

"Now," he said to Alicia, "what was I saying?"

"That you gave Mr. Soupcon a lecture, Uncle."

"Yes, yes. And when I was finished, the young rapscallion had the audacity to say that it had all been a mistake and that, far from being guilty, he should, at this very moment, be receiving my commendations."

"And on what account, sir?" Alicia said quickly, seeing Imogene open her mouth and hoping to prevent any further insults.

"Why," Sir Humphrey said, "it was the young gentleman's claim that he was walking along the North Parade at midnight when he came upon an altercation. A gentleman of his own age, apparently in a drunken condition, was, for no apparent reason, engaged in attempting to take old Pilchorn's stick away from him. Mr. Soupcon claims that he entered the fray with the intention of protecting the watchman and that the other gentleman, having succeeded in breaking the stick over his knee, departed."

"Whereupon," Imogene interrupted in a dry voice, "old Pilchorn turned around and arrested the very person who had come to his defense. Yes, I have no doubt that *was* the case. It is as logical as most things."

"According to Pilchorn, miss, one person attacked him, one person broke his stick, and one person was arrested. And they were all one and the same, in a word, Mr. Soupcon."

The father turned. The daughter did likewise. In an attempt to ward off a direct confrontation which was bound to be of an unpleasant nature, Alicia took the floor.

"And am I right in assuming, sir," she said, "that Randolph is Mr. Soupcon's friend and that he is trying to defend him?"

"If it were that simple, gel, do you think I would have been thrown into this state?" Sir Humphrey demanded, bounding out of his chair, his face a mask of misery. "You might as well know it all. The truth will out no matter how I try to suppress it. And the truth is this. My son—my only son and heir—has sworn that he was the very man Mr. Soupcon saw attacking the watchman on the North Parade."

CHAPTER THREE

At about ten o'clock of any morning, it was customary for everyone of any consequence in Bath to make the daily migration to the Pump Room, where the waters might be taken and an excellent view was provided of the King's Bath, where those who preferred an exterior tonic frolicked in the hot water which bubbled from the underground springs first discovered by the Romans.

"I'm going to see to it myself that you take the plunge one of these days, Imogene," Randolph declared as he stood between his sister and Alicia and watched a horse-faced lady, outfitted in a canvas overall, allow herself to be helped down into the steaming water by a pinched-skinned attendant. As soon as the lady was submerged, the canvas cover came floating up like a balloon to the surface, causing two younger gentlemen situated nearby to make an exchange of comments behind their hands and break into salacious laughter.

"It's quite disgusting," Imogene said, turning her back on the scene. "If people were meant to bathe in public, they would have been provided with fins."

"Alicia finds it all quite amusing," Randolph declared, glancing at his cousin who was, in fact, smiling to see the horse-faced lady below her point her finger at the two young gentlemen and deliver herself of what appeared to be a number of sharp words before allowing the attendant to deal with the problem of the canvas.

"I will not have Alicia thrown in my face at every opportunity," Imogene retorted. "Alicia this. Alicia that. Why, my father is quite besotted with her, and even Mama allows her liberties. And now you . . ."

She did not speak with the intention of having Alicia hear, however, and with this in mind had led her brother a few feet away, thus providing all the distance needed in a room so crowded that the sound which arose from it was like the chatter of thousands of starlings.

"It's not Alicia you're angry with," Randolph said laconically. He was a tall, narrow fellow with the complexion of a girl and a tentative expression in his blue eyes. It was Alicia's private opinion that the sophistication which he assumed was no more than skin deep and that, although he dressed himself with the flair of a macaroni, he was, in fact, a rather simple fellow and weak-willed to boot. All of which was not to say that he was anything but a perfectly charming companion.

"I know," Imogene muttered. "The fact of the

matter is that I am much annoyed with *you*, Randolph. How could you have been so very foolish?"

Few people could resist Randolph's smile, and Imogene was not one of them. "At least," she murmured, "you might try to explain. I mean to say, you don't know how difficult it is for me to try to defend you to Papa—or to Mama, for that matter—when I do not have the facts at hand."

"Poor Imogene," Randolph replied. "Very well. Let the three of us take one of the tables in the corner and have a little chat. Come along, Alicia. There are as many foolish foibles to observe inside this room as there are in the bath below. Did you hear me tell my dear sister that I am about to make a clean breast of my crimes?"

They made a handsome picture as they traversed the long room, and not a few eyes turned to follow them. True it was that Imogene was dressed with her usual restraint in a fine contrast to the London ladies with their carefully arranged dishabille, their paint and patches, and their towering, befeathered turbans. Alicia too was more modestly dressed, preferring mobcap to a wig or turban of a morning, but it was a consequence that her bright red curls tangled themselves on the shoulders of her emerald-green gown, giving her a kind of glitter which made the ladies' eyes narrow and raised the quizzing glass to more than one gentleman's eye. As for Randolph, youth and handsomeness combined with dress which was in the very pink of fashion was quite sufficient reason for him to attract a following of his own.

"Here, now. This will do, I think," he said when they had finally found three empty seats together about a round table. "But, I say, sir. Are you with anyone? Do you mind if we share a table?"

The gentleman who rose and bowed let his dark eyes flicker over the three young people and inclined his head in mute permission before retaking his chair. Alicia thought that she had never seen such a powerful face. The bones were prominent, the mouth a fine-cut line. His skin was so dark that the contrast to his white wig, like that one worn by Randolph, was great enough to give one pause. He looked like someone who had recently come back from foreign climes, and although his blue jacket of superfine, his riding breeches, and polished Hessian boots were quite within the current style, there was an air about him of one who found his surroundings curious in the extreme and not, perhaps, particularly pleasant. At all events his chair was pushed away from the table, and he was clearly so intent on observing the Pump Room crush that they could speak as though they were private. At least this was what Randolph promptly proceeded to do with his usual frank air.

"Now, cousin," he said to Alicia. "Imogene insists on knowing the truth about my behavior on what Papa refers to as 'the night in question,' when Soupcon, like the valiant chap he is, rescued me from an extremely awkward situation. Tell me, will it be a bore for you if I explain it to her, or will you take your usual stance and be amused?"

Alicia moved her seat in such a way as to put her back to the stranger who shared their table. There was something about him which disturbed her, even though it was clear that he took no interest either in her or in her cousins.

"Whichever way the story affects me, I will neither yawn nor titter," she assured Randolph. "But I will tell you this. I would not be human if I did not want to know what my own cousin was doing on the North Parade at midnight, breaking a watchman's stick."

"An *old* watchman's stick," Imogene said grimly. "Oh, Randolph, how could you do such a thing?"

"Why, as to breaking the stick, that was very easy," her brother told her. "What is more difficult is to explain precisely why I did it."

"You had been drinking?"

"I expect I must have been, since, the following morning, I had only a vague memory of the proceedings. It was only when poor Soupcon sent a message to me from the roundhouse that I realized what had happened. As I told Papa, it was only right that I pay the fine, although, I must confess, he was very reluctant to loan me the money to do so until I told him that unless he saw his way clear to doing so I would have to make a public confession of the fact that it was I and not

Soupcon who was guilty of breaking the king's peace."

"You mean," Imogene said, wide-eyed, "that Papa sentenced someone and then paid their fine in order to protect his own son!"

"Somehow it doesn't sound like such an excellent thing when you put it that way," Randolph reflected. "But that's more or less what it amounts to, dashed if it ain't."

"Only fancy that Papa would do such a thing!" Imogene cried. "And him a justice of the peace, always talking about right and wrong and black and white. Why, I declare, I never thought he could be such a hypocrite!"

"My dear cousin," Alicia said quickly, unable to remain silent any longer. "You are very hard on your papa, I think. All of us make mistakes, and sometimes one of them complements the other."

"Always the peacemaker," Randolph said, laughing in his charming way.

Alicia turned on him. "And you, sir," she retorted, "have come out of this scot-free. It is your admission, is it not, that you attacked an elderly watchman and proceeded to break his nightstick!"

"That is what Soupcon claims," Randolph told her with mock ruefulness. "And I must take his word for it since, as you know, I . . ."

"You were in your cups," Alicia interrupted. "You tell us that as though it excused anything. Is the simple matter of a gentleman's drunken-

36

ness enough to excuse him from every enormity."

"I scarcely think that breaking a stick could be classified as an enormity," Randolph replied. "But I take your general drift, cousin. No. It would be wrong, I expect, to hide behind a glass of spirits. But the fact is, I do *not* recall what happened."

"Can this fellow Soupcon be relied upon to be telling the truth?" Alicia demanded.

"As much as any other of my friends," Randolph told her. "Which is not saying much, I know, but I do not think that any one of them would lie to get another one of us in trouble. There is a certain amount of esprit de corps, as the Frenchies say."

There was about Randolph such a combination of the repugnant and the appealing as to make Alicia wonder how it was that so many contrary elements should hide behind such a handsome face.

"Well then," she said. "We must assume he told the truth. By that I mean Soupcon. But that because of something in his general appearance, your papa decided . . ."

"Decided not to hear the evidence complete," Imogene declared, slapping the palm of her hand against the flat top of the table in a manner which, if not particularly delicate, was expressive enough. "I know that you are trying to smooth things over, Alicia, but I really do not think you can. Mr. Soupcon tried to explain. If Papa had given him the opportunity, he could have called Randolph . . ."

"Called the judge's own son to give evidence before the bar!" Randolph scoffed. "I'll give you that Soupcon isn't the brightest chap alive, but he's brighter than that, I assure you."

"You mean to say you do not think Papa would have accepted your confession?"

"Why should he have?" Randolph demanded. "Everything was going along swimmingly. An old man with a sad story and a broken nightstick to back it up. Not to mention a lantern. For the life of me I cannot remember a lantern. Anyway, he has the watchman and he has the suspect. Furthermore, the suspect has clearly had a glass or two and does not look Papa straight in the eyes. Always a damning sign that. Do you think Soupcon would have been patted on the back if he had declared that I and not he was the miscreant who was wanted? Why, instead of being clapped in the roundhouse until he could pay his fine, he might have been put in pillory. Sent to prison. Deported!"

"Pray do not exaggerate," Alicia murmured. "And lower your voice, cousin. It is all very well for you to criticize your father, but I do not think you care to be overheard."

"Why, everyone knows what the courts are," Randolph announced. "If you are poor and cannot pay the fine, then you are sent off to the roundhouse or worse without a mite of evidence against you. And if, as in Soupcon's case, you do not appear trustworthy, you will be put to some inconvenience, at least. But have a wealthy man of title, let us say, come to the bar, and you will find that very little trouble is taken to prove him guilty. Indeed, the exact opposite may well be true. Ah, if you are looking for hypocrisy, go to the church, and if you want injustice, go to the courts. That is what I tried to tell Papa, but he was unreasonable enough to offer to strike me down where I stood if I persisted."

"Papa is so conservative," Imogene agreed. "He never sees the need for reform."

"My dear cousins," Alicia said with a glance over her shoulder. The dark-skinned gentleman did not appear to be listening, for his deep-set eyes still skimmed the motley crowd, but she had an uncomfortable feeling that he was paying more attention to their conversation than she would like. "I do not think you ought to be so eager to criticize your father."

"We only want to help him see the error of his ways," Imogene declared. "I do not blame him precisely, you understand. He practices justice as does everyone else of his position in this country. Indeed, I expect that he is fairer than some, by far. Why, I heard the other day that when a gentleman was brought before the justice at Bristol and tried to defend himself, he was told: 'You are an Irishman, sir, and that is always sufficient evidence with me.' And with that he was forthwith dispatched to Canada.'"

"And it is not as though there was nothing but

intolerance and snobbery to deal with," Randolph continued more seriously than Alicia had ever seen him before. "I have not accused Papa of being corrupt. But there are many justices who are. Not to mention constables, turnkeys, and watchmen, as well. As I put it to Soupcon when I paid his fine . . ."

Alicia knew him too well to be taken in, although Imogene was staring at her brother adoringly. Randolph often had these fits of enthusiasm. Just now he saw himself as a reformer of the courts. Next week would find him in another role. When Alicia had arrived at Bath, his main enthusiasm had been the doing away of certain regulations imposed a decade or more before by Beau Nash during his days as social arbiter of Bath, including the relaxation of certain rules which governed gambling. Her cousin was appealing in many ways, but he was not one to follow a set course for long, and Alicia could only hope that he would keep his criticism of his father to himself before he caused a scandal.

She started when the dark gentleman who shared their table spoke.

"Permit me to introduce myself," he said abruptly, rising. "I am Captain Gerard Hillary, only recently become the editor of the Bath *Gazette* on the death of my uncle. I fear I could not help but overhear a few scraps of your conversation, sir, and, I must confess, my curiosity has been piqued. You are, I take it, interested in reform?"

"I am indeed," Randolph said, also rising, his girl's complexion turning pink. "Allow me to present my sister and my cousin, Miss . . ."

"Yes, yes," the captain said as though such introductions were an annoying interruption. "But I wonder if we could not profitably speak privately, sir. I have a certain proposition which I would like to put before you."

Alicia gripped her cousin's arm. "Stop him," she whispered. "For heaven's sake, do something before it is too late."

But, having begged leave to quit them, Randolph was already gone. He and the stranger vanished like smoke into the crowd.

"Well," Imogene said defiantly, "you can pull a face if you like, cousin, but I think Randolph should feel complimented. Newspaper editors are important men. And Captain Hillary is most impressive."

"And dangerous," Alicia murmured. "I think he is the most dangerous-looking man I have ever seen."

CHAPTER FOUR

Because of Sir Humphrey's profession as magistrate, it was only fitting that he should have a residence close to the center of the town for the purpose of making him accessible, it being the habit of the time for him to conduct a good deal of his business in offices in his own house. This was one of the many subjects which set Imogene to railing, for it was her conviction that the only proper place to live in Bath was one of the adjoining white Palladian structures which lined the Royal Crescent.

"Besides, the air is better on the hill," she was fond of saying, giving a little cough. "It is a wonder that my lungs have not been affected, living straight beside the river. But then, Mama has never been concerned with anyone besides herself, and as for Papa, I declare, he would probably be perfectly content to live in a cave somewhere, as long as there were cases to be tried and felons to be convicted."

As a consequence of this dissatisfaction with the town, Imogene would often persuade Alicia to climb the steep, cobbled Gay Street to the Circus and from there, to the left, to the Royal Crescent, where the windows of the graceful houses with their columned porches looked out onto a greensward which had become something of a rustic park with great elm trees all about it and a few sheep grazing, to crop the grass.

"I am determined to marry someone who lives there," Imogene announced as the two girls walked together on the hillside overlooking the town and river. "That is my only prerequisite, I assure you. If he possesses a house on the Royal Crescent, any gentleman may have me."

Alicia threw back her head and laughed, for although her cousin's outrageous statements threw her mother into a frenzy and her father into a fit of rage, she found them amusing, all of which seemed to suit Imogene very well.

"Laugh away," her cousin told her now, "but you will see how serious I am one day. At present the only unmarried possibility is young Soupcon."

"The one who was arrested by the watchman?" Alicia asked her, as, arm in arm, they turned to walk in another direction.

The two girls made a pretty picture in their morning gowns, for both of them wore a polonaise to suit the latest fashion with skirts which rose above their ankles, and small hoops covered with flouncing petticoats covered overskirts which fell in folds from the waist. Imogene wore blue over white and Alicia green and white stripes. Each of them wore a tulle neckerchief crossed at the bodice, and this modesty extended to their heads, where each covered some part of her curls with a white dormeuse with a loose-fitting crown thickly fringed with lace and decorated with a bow. The graceful way they had of walking completed the appeal.

"His father, who is a viscount, lives in that house over there," Imogene said, pointing, which was perfectly proper since there was no one else about. "The sixth house from the left. Of course, that is the difficulty. As long as Lord Soupcon is alive, the house will remain in his possession, and since the son is a scamp and a rascal . . ."

"Pray be serious, Cousin!" Alicia declared. The afternoon breeze had flushed her ivory skin and ruffled the red curls which had escaped her cap. "If you persist in going on in this absurd fashion, you may come to believe yourself."

Imogene threw her a wicked glance and then, her attention distracted, began to wave her handkerchief about. Looking back toward the Crescent, Alicia saw that Randolph was in the process of descending from a sedan chair carried by four hulking fellows, one of whom spat after the young gentleman when he had handed him a coin and set off to join his sister on the grass.

"Randolph *will* always take a chair when he comes up here to see Soupcon," Imogene declared with an impatient note in her voice. "And he never will tip properly. I like to tell him that it is all very well for someone as young as he to

44

take a chair when it is raining, but that simply to negotiate a hill . . ."

Alicia found that she could not attend to her cousin's pronouncements. Ever since this morning when Randolph had gone off with Captain Hillary, she had been conscious of a vague anxiety. Randolph was a weak creature in many ways, and he could so easily allow himself to be led into some trouble or other. Besides, what would a man like Captain Hillary want with someone like Randolph? He knew nothing of him except what he had overheard when they had all shared a table.

She had tried all day to recollect precisely what that had been. Randolph had told his account of the incident with the watchman to the effect that his own father had been guilty of punishing the wrong man to protect his own son. And, as she recalled it, he had then gone on to present his opinion of the court system in general, not using complimentary terms. She was certain that the captain, although he had pretended not to, had listened closely, and she was equally certain that what he had heard had persuaded him that Randolph could be useful in some way or other. And so, while Imogene continued to fuss about her brother's habits, Alicia watched him come toward them, a foppish figure dressed in the latest fashion, with a sense of premonition.

"'Pon my soul, I did not expect to see you!" Randolph exclaimed. "I came along to visit Soupcon and tell him the good news."

"Has it something to do with the proposition Captain Hillary said that he meant to put to you?" Alicia demanded.

"Damme, Cousin, you are very clever," Randolph told her with a grin, clasping his hands together under the tails of his blue coat. "Mind, this is to be a secret. On no account is Papa to know."

Imogene indicated her pleasure with a little cheer, not at all of the sort suitable to a lady, and announced that secrets from her father were her favorite sort.

"I am to provide information for the newspaper," Randolph continued proudly. "Here now! There's Soupcon out on the street! I can't let him get away!"

Eager to hear the remainder of the story, the two girls followed him, skirts billowing, up to the Crescent itself, where young Soupcon was just setting out in the direction of the town. He was an insouciant-looking fellow, who clearly prided himself on being a dandy. He wore a club-style wig, in the manner of the members of the Macaroni Club in London, on top of which he wore a tiny tricorne hat, which he proceeded to lift now, in greeting, with the tip of his gold-knobbed walking cane. His breeches fitted him so tightly that it seemed certain that they would burst if he ever had reason to break into a run, and his coat and waistcoat were very short. His fanciful appearance was completed by his red and white striped stockings and red-heeled shoes.

"Struth if I hadn't thought to find you at the Assembly Hall," he announced to Randolph in a voice which was only a trifle shrill. "We had a game of whist arranged there this afternoon, if you remember."

"Why, as for that," Randolph told him proudly, "I am now a working man." There followed a pause then for young Soupcon to express his amazement, and then, at last, the story came pouring out.

It seemed that the captain had taken Randolph to his offices in a building not far from the North Parade. The printing press was located there, and men had been working. Clearly Randolph had been struck by the businesslike atmosphere and had apparently listened with some attention as Captain Hillary had told him something about the publishing process.

But another subject had soon claimed their attention. The captain, it seemed, was intent on instituting judicial reform. It was his personal conviction that a great many changes could be made, that, in fact, there were more serious crimes abroad than the court took notice of, and that what criminal activity there was observed was prosecuted in an uneven manner.

"And what did you tell him?" Alicia demanded, as soon as her cousin gave her the opportunity to insert a word.

"Why, what *could* I tell him when he said that he thought I was just the man to help him," Randolph declared, throwing out his unsubstantial

47

chest. "I agreed to assist him in any way I can. For a price, of course. I am no fool, I assure you. And he has promised to be generous. We shook hands on it."

Alicia waited until Imogene had extended her congratulations and calculated the effect all this would have on her father, which speculation was followed by Randolph's explanation that he would not be able to be as useful to the captain as he could be if his "position," as he called it, was of general knowledge. In particular his father, as magistrate, must not be told.

"But what *is* it precisely that you are to do?" Alicia demanded.

"Why, I am to provide information," Randolph told her, at which young Soupcon called him a gudgeon and clapped him on the back with so much enthusiasm that one of the two fobs which Randolph had attached to his waistcoat fell off and a scramble followed to retrieve it from the gutter.

"What sort of information?" Alicia inquired, at the tag end of her patience. It was difficult for her to believe that her cousin could have allowed himself to be taken in so easily. Clearly he thought, somehow, that a natural talent—although Alicia could not guess what that could be—had recommended him to Captain Hillory, while on the contrary, it was apparent that, having sized him up at the Pump Room that morning and having determined that his father was magistrate, the captain had decided to take whatever advantage of the young man that he could.

"This and that," Randolph said with a shrug of his thin shoulders. "Whatever I think may be useful. And, of course, if any of my friends were to come to me with information, I would not forget to be generous."

With this announcement, he looked meaningfully at young Soupcon who, in turn, looked at Imogene, who . . .

"You mean to say you have become a paid informer?" Alicia demanded. "Someone who picks up whispers and repeats them for this—this adventurer to print?"

"I do not think you should call Captain Hillary an adventurer," Randolph said, drawing himself up very straight.

"He seemed to me to have a great deal of dignity," Imogene contributed, tossing her fair curls. "Even better, he is handsome and there is an air of mystery about him."

"His skin is dark enough to be a farmer's," young Soupcon declared with a faint touch of complaint entering his voice, as though he was not glad to hear Imogene so fulsome in her praise of the stranger.

"That is because he was in the campaigns in America," Randolph explained.

"I expect he told you all about his bravery and the suffering he endured," Alicia murmured resentfully. She knew her cousin well enough to know that, although feckless, he would probably be difficult to dissuade on this occasion. Particularly if he found a great deal about the captain to admire.

"Indeed, he only mentioned it in passing," Randolph told her. "He is no braggart. I am certain of it. He has sincere convictions concerning the law, and I intend to assist him in his endeavors in any way I can."

"I declare, I never expected to hear you talk about convictions!" Imogene told her brother as they all stepped back to avoid a passing barouche which had come lumbering along like a great, black beetle on the crescent road. "You cannot persuade me that you are doing this because you have discovered principles, at last."

"I made no claim to anything of the sort," Randolph told her haughtily. "The captain is a man I can admire. And he intends to pay me very well indeed. He assured me that any details I should hear from my father would be useful to him, and that . . ."

"Any details!" Alicia cried, whirling up to her cousin with her gloved hands clenched. Anger had dyed her cheeks scarlet, and her green eyes sparkled. "Why, the gentleman is asking you to tell him things about your own father which he will then proceed to use against him! Among other things, apparently he intends to criticize the court. And the court in this town *is* your father! How could you have even entertained the idea that you would help him?"

Randolph had the decency to look disconcerted, at least. "Well," he muttered, scuffing at the ground. "This case with Soupcon here was an example of how far my father can go wrong. And you cannot say that I have not tried to reason with him, for I have, time and again. He is unfair and he knows it, and he will make no defense. At least he will not make one to me. *I* am considered beneath his notice. *I* only exist to be criticized. Well, I'll be a jackanape if we won't see!"

Even Imogene joined Alicia in looking appalled. Neither of them had realized, until this moment, how deeply ingrained Randolph's rebellion had become, how much he resented Sir Humphrey with his blast and bluster and his constant complaints. Alicia had come to think that the constant snits and snats father and son fell into were a form of habit each had become accustomed to. If they constantly berated one another, that was only because that was the way in which they had settled on communicating. But she had underestimated their differences, she saw now, although Randolph was trying to put a good face on it.

"Of course I will not make any serious trouble for Papa," he said in a strained, lighthearted manner. "In matter of fact, I think that I will spend most of my time concentrating on crime. If there is an underground ring of criminals in this city, I intend to uncover it directly."

"Even though there may be danger?" his sister cried, clutching at his elbow.

"'Pon my soul, you *are* a bang-up fellow!" young Soupcon exclaimed.

"Not to mention a fool, to boot," Alicia said, but in such a low murmur that she was not heard, particularly since Randolph had begun to declaim loudly about the need to fetch a sedan chair to take him down the hill and into town.

CHAPTER FIVE

It soon became clear that Captain Hillary was making no secret of his intentions. That evening, on account of Sir Humphrey demanding that they remain at home, Lady Fairbreaks worked her way into a temper, which she was clever enough, however, to disguise. Alicia saw, as soon as she had come down the stairs to join them about the fire, that her aunt meant to take her revenge by making the evening as uncomfortable as possible for her husband.

"I spent the afternoon with Mrs. Tanner," she announced to the room in general, providing her as it did with an audience of three: Imogene, who was having a fit of grumbles due to being forced to remain at home, and was, accordingly, sitting in the corner looking put-upon; Alicia, who was trying her hand at some embroidery in an effort to demonstrate that she did not mind being domestic; and Sir Humphrey himself, who was hunched up in a wing chair with his nose in *The Gazette.*

"Dear Dorine allows herself to be so put-upon

by her husband and those frightful children," Lady Fairbreaks continued, pitching her voice at just that level which made it impossible to ignore, even though Alicia's uncle bravely made the effort. "She never has her way with things. Only today she was complaining because her husband did not want to go to the concert. Every Wednesday it is the same. He simply will not go. And her sons are harum-scarum. Off in every direction. One never knows what they are up to."

Nothing was said, Alicia noted, of the fact that Randolph had made his getaway, muttering something about important business as he sped out of the house. She knew by now that one of the many purposes which her aunt's friendship with Mrs. Tanner filled was to allow Lady Fairbreaks to benefit by any comparisons which might be made between them, comparisons which were too numerous to mention, the most obvious being that Mrs. Tanner was indeed a subdued little creature with a mousey aspect to her. Indeed, whenever Alicia saw her, she always had the impression that given the slightest disturbance, the lady would scuttle away to a hole.

"Dear Dorine," Lady Fairbreaks continued, "I told her that she should assert herself more. Of course, nothing can be done about her looks. *That,* at least, is quite a hopeless matter. One would never think that only a single year divides us, since I look so much the younger. Don't you agree, my dear?"

Sir Humphrey grumbled something and buried himself even further in his newspaper, while Lady Fairbreaks, who was sitting opposite him, cleared her throat in order to speak more loudly still.

"Dear Dorine," she said with admirable persistence. "I said to her, 'If I do not go to the concert this evening, it is because I do not care to go. *My* husband is always ready to bend his wishes to suit mine. *My* husband only wants to make me happy. *My* husband . . .'"

"Damme, woman!" Sir Humphrey cried. "Have done with it! Have done!"

Alicia found herself making an involuntary comparison between this household and the one that she had so lately come from. Never in her wildest fancies could she imagine her mother and her father speaking to one another in this way. In the first place they were both perfectly content, of an evening after evensong, to stroll together down the hedgerowed lane which led between the church and vicarage, stopping at various cottages along the way to talk with friends and neighbors. Indeed, in her letters to them, she had not made a point of being exact about the amount of going out which was required of her. She was not certain if her mother would think it was quite wholesome to be every morning at the Pump Room and from there to hurry to the library and the shops. As for going to the abbey church at noontime, her father would agree that that was commendable only as long as he did not realize that everyone went there to be seen. The amount of food served at three would appall both her parents, and as for attending either a ball, a concert, or a private soirée of some sort every night of the week, surely they had never thought of such activity when they had sent her off to join her aunt and uncle.

But Alicia admitted she had enjoyed herself. And now she knew that so much socializing could become a habit which was difficult to break. Clearly Imogene, for example, was in extreme discomfort at the thought of spending an entire evening before the family hearth, and Lady Fairbreaks was taking her revenge in a ruthless fashion. As for herself, Alicia found that she, too, missed the excitement, and warned herself that she must become careful of this life. She did not care to look forward to a future of the furious activity her aunt and cousins seemed to enjoy.

Her contemplation was disturbed by a dreadful roar from Sir Humphrey, who, starting to his feet, flung the paper to the floor. Rather than acknowledge that anything was wrong, Lady Fairbreaks turned to Imogene and observed that she seemed very cheerful this evening, whereupon her daughter rose and scowled her way out of the room. As for Alicia, she was not quite certain what her role should be in this distracted household, and for lack of a ready answer, applied herself to her embroidery in a more certain fashion.

"Damme, I want to know what that fellow

thinks that he is doing," Sir Humphrey demanded.

Rather than give him the satisfaction of being noticed, Lady Fairbreaks observed that Alicia had woven a pretty pattern. She herself was a marvel with a needle, although lately she scarcely ever found the time. And, of course, when she was Alicia's age, she had such an endless line of suitors that . . .

"I said I want to know what that fellow thinks he's doing," her husband demanded for a second time, with such a face of thunder that even Lady Fairbreaks was obliged to give him mind.

"I am sure that if you do not know, my dear," she said in her florid manner, "I would not presume to guess."

"Damme, you do not even know who I am making reference to, madam," Sir Humphrey told her.

But it soon became apparent that Lady Fairbreaks was determined not to ask. Instead she noted that she could not remember when she had so much enjoyed an evening and hoped that they would have many others like it. At which her husband bellowed his impatience and, thrusting the newspaper before her, drew her attention to a name.

"Why, if you mean Captain Hillary, my dear," Alicia's aunt told him, "I am sure you should have said so at the start. I am as much concerned as you are at the changes he seems determined to make. I hear he is determined to reduce the social notices quite by half. What we will do when we are not informed who is down from London and who is ready to depart, I'm sure I do not know. However, I admit that I am puzzled that the length of the social column should mean as much to you as it appears to do.".

"I have no care for social columns, madam!" Sir Humphrey exclaimed, clearly quite beside himself. "It is what he means to take their place with that I do not like."

"Well, as for that, I know nothing of it," Lady Fairbreaks declared. "You know, my dear, that I never read any other section of the paper. What he intends to do with his precious columns is quite beneath my notice, I assure you. Alicia, do you really think that you should use that shade of pink? Scarlet would be a good deal better for the rose, I assure you. Something on the shade of your uncle's face."

"We are not discussing my face, madam," Sir Humphrey shouted.

"It will serve as well as any other subject for a quiet domestic evening," Lady Fairbreaks told him. "You know that the doctor told you . . ."

"My doctor has nothing to do with this matter!" her husband told her in exasperation. "You will oblige me by keeping to the subject."

Lady Fairbreaks beamed up at him. "Why, how can I, sir, when I do not even know what the subject is? Are we to play at conundrums? If we are, we must have Imogene back. How glad I am that you would not have us go out to the concert, sir."

Alicia was afraid that her uncle would resort to violence. Indeed, she would not much have blamed him if he had.

"This fellow Hillary intends to make an examination of the way in which law is administered in this city, madam!" Sir Humphrey exclaimed. "And he implies—just here in this article—that there is substantial reason for reform. Put it another way, he intends to attack me. Why, if ever I have heard a battle cry . . ."

"La, my dear, the gentleman is a military man," Lady Fairbreaks told him. "What else but battle cries can you expect?"

Sir Humphrey ignored the comment. "Furthermore," he roared, "he claims that Bath is crime-riddled. He claims there is an underground and that he intends to expose it. He means to intrude himself on my province, and that is something I will not allow!"

Alicia no longer made any claim to attending to her embroidery and let the hoop fall to her lap. Clearly this was going to be worse than she had expected. What would happen when Sir Humphrey discovered, as he was sure to in the end, that his own son had been enlisted by the enemy? Clearly all this was bound to end in catastrophe. And Captain Hillary, dark and handsome, had been the one to start it. He had stirred waters which, although never quiet, had not, at least, been turbulent.

"Well, as for what you will or will not allow, my dear," Lady Fairbreaks replied, "I can make no comment. As I was saying to Mrs. Tanner this very afternoon . . ."

"What do I care what you said to Mrs. Tanner?" Sir Humphrey told her. "I have been put in an awkward position, indeed, and you intend to make no comment!"

"Only fancy that I could ever have wished to attend a concert," Alicia's aunt observed. "I declare that this is much more exciting! Particularly since I do not think that Captain Hillary, from all that I have heard about him, is the sort to change his mind about anything once he has settled on it."

Sir Humphrey hovered over her like a dark red cloud. Anger seemed to diminish rather than enlarge him, and his blue satin coat and embroidered waistcoat seemed about to fall off him.

"What do you know about the fellow, madam?" he demanded. "I know all too well how assiduously you collect idle gossip. What can you tell me about him? You will oblige me by not playing games!"

"Games, sir!" Lady Fairbreaks replied. "Why, I never play them. And since you have never liked to listen to my gossip, I do not think anything I would have to say on the subject of Captain Hillary would interest you."

Alicia's aunt had chosen to wear a sack-backed gown of purple patterned silk for this domestic evening. Her square décolletage was cut very low indeed, and, in the heat of battle—for battle it was, Alicia decided, her bosom heaved in a substantial manner. Her dearest aim, no doubt, was to have her husband beg her for information, and this, to his humiliation, he was forced to do.

"What do you know about him?" Sir Humphrey said, subsiding in the chair.

"Only tittle-tattle, my dear," Lady Fairbreaks said blandly. "Nothing that would interest you."

How surely she knew how to punish him, Alicia thought with a pang. She was learning a good deal more about life than she suspected that her parents had ever wanted her to do. Was this what happened to most marriages? Did they become battlegrounds on which there could never be enough gore to satisfy? In time, would she become one of this number? Shrill and harsh? Enjoying the pain she managed to administer? What sort of world was this that she had entered? She would have liked to depart from the scene, but something held her.

"Anything would interest me, my dear," Sir Humphrey said, reclining in his chair as though to acknowledge his defeat. For the first time since she had come to Bath, Alicia pitied him. For all his bluff and bluster, he was clearly no match for Lady Fairbreaks.

"Well, in that event," her aunt proceeded, clearly satisfied that she had won the match, "I can tell you that it is reported that the captain is not a man to easily be thwarted. Although, perhaps, that is not precisely what you wished to hear. They say that he was something of a hero in America. And when he came here to take over his uncle's newspaper, he made it clear that he intended to make an example of this city."

"An example!" Sir Humphrey said in a voice which was more of a wail than a bellow. "Surely not. I will not allow it!"

"I think you cannot prevent it, my dear," his wife responded in a cheerful sort of way. "The newspaper is his to do with as he wants. Although I do wish that he would give a second thought to the social column. Indeed, I think that I will ask him here for an evening in order to convince him . . ."

"I will not have him in my house, madam!" Sir Humphrey declared.

"Well, I will have him in mine, sir," Lady Fairbreaks replied in a cheerful manner. "You can make yourself absent for the evening, if you prefer. But I must do what I think is best in preserving the amenities and . . ."

"Amenities be damned, madam!" Sir Humphrey cried. But it was the cry of a drowning swimmer who knows that all is lost.

Alicia gathered up her embroidery at this point and hurriedly left the room with a murmured apology, which she knew that neither one of them would listen to. All that she knew was that she could not bear to meet Captain Hillary in this house or, for that matter, in any other, knowing, as she did, what he intended to do.

CHAPTER SIX

During the days which followed, Randolph was noticeably absent from the Fairbreaks household. Otherwise, life went on much as usual, with the single exception that Sir Humphrey seemed to be prosecuting an increasing number of people. In the mornings promptly at seven, they would be brought before him from the roundhouse, petty criminals of all varieties in shabby clothing and with the hangdog look of those who have taken a risk and lost.

Lady Fairbreaks was proud enough that her husband was a magistrate, but the daily nitty-gritty of his business was something that she made a point to avoid. It had been at her insistence that a doorway had been cut into his offices from the side of the house which faced an alley, down which the miscreants came and went. But despite the increased pace of his prosecutions, Sir Humphrey never spoke of them. Instead, he could be heard every evening now grumbling over his paper, and once Alicia heard him mutter, apropos of what she was not certain, that that fellow had better keep his distance from the court.

As for Lady Fairbreaks, she had been quite successful in demonstrating to her husband that her evenings, at least, were far better not spent at home. As a consequence Alicia and Imogene resumed their round of balls and soirées, and Alicia declared herself relieved that on none of these occasions did their path cross that of Captain Hillary, for she knew that were she to see him she might not be able to restrain the indignation which she felt over his having taken such advantage of her cousin.

"I do not think that it is fair of Randolph not to tell us precisely what he is doing!" Imogene began to say with increasing frequency. Whenever possible, she waylaid her brother and demanded to know what he was up to. But weak-charactered as Randolph was in most things, he proved himself stubborn enough in this. He would admit that he was acting as Captain Hillary's agent, but he would say nothing of his activities, except to imply that he was "onto" something of the utmost importance, something which would shake the town to its foundations when the truth was known.

"He will get himself into serious trouble," Imogene complained. "You do not know as well as I do, Alicia, what a witless creature he can be. I am certain that he is involved with some unscrupulous characters who will take advantage of him. At first I thought that it was all exciting, but that was when I did not think that he would make a mystery of it. I must find out what he is doing, and you will help me."

And, when Alicia assured her cousin that what she did or did not do would be dependent on the sense of it, Imogene fell into a temper, which Alicia left her to indulge in at her leisure, it having been her observation that her cousin restrained herself in direct relation to the number of her audience.

But when Imogene, repentant, came to Alicia to suggest that they approach Soupcon to discover what he knew about Randolph's mysterious activities, Alicia was glad enough to agree. However, their hopes in this direction floundered when it appeared that even young Soupcon, insouciant as he was in most matters of public concern, told them that his lips were sealed and promptly demonstrated the fact by contorting his face in such a manner that people who passed them on the street turned back to look.

That evening when they attended the dancing at the Assembly Hall located closest to the North Parade, Imogene was in a strangely pensive condition. Usually she approached such evenings with fresh enthusiasm, asking any unfamiliar partner whom she might garner whether or not he maintained a residence on the Royal Crescent. But tonight her heart was not in the business, and Alicia was afraid that she could guess at the general nature of the thoughts which were crossing her cousin's mind. She had lived in the Fairbreaks household long enough to know that neither Imogene nor Randolph went for long without what they wanted. And if Imogene wanted to find out what her brother was doing, she would find a way.

As a consequence Alicia was doubly startled when she saw Captain Hillary come into the hall. It was the first time she had seen him at any such entertainment, and he looked as alien, somehow, as he had looked that morning in the Pump Room. It was as though he were a traveler in a strange land who showed a certain restrained curiosity, but could be trusted to make no effort to join the natives in their peculiar ways. Indeed, Alicia thought as her sense of outrage grew and expanded, he could only have come here this evening to gather some information which he could use in an editorial, some carp or criticism of their ways. She flushed when suddenly his dark eyes caught hers and he came across the dance floor to where she was waiting for her last partner to bring her a glass of punch.

"Miss Eaton," he said with a bow, "no doubt you have forgotten me, but we met nearly a week ago at the Pump Room."

She had forgotten how he disturbed her. It was not simply that he was handsome, or that the darkness of his skin made such a dramatic contrast with his powdered hair. There was some other quality about him which made her restless, and this, joined to her anger, made her answer him in a way she never had intended to.

"I am not in the least likely to forget you, sir," she told him, "since you have been responsible for placing my cousin in an awkward situation."

He moved his mouth in such a way as to tell her that he, too, was quick to anger. "I assure you, Miss Eaton," he replied, "that I have not the slightest notion of what you are making reference to. If your cousin is, as you say, in an awkward condition, than it must be of his own making, for I do not pretend to influence any single individual's life."

Alicia could feel that she was flushing. "If by that, sir, you intend to remind me of the power of your editorial writing, I cannot see that it has left much mark. Life goes on in Bath much as it did before."

His dark eyes were curious. "And you approve of that?" he demanded. "Or do you know so little about it that you could not possibly make an honest judgment?"

That last was so near the line that Alicia felt disconcerted. What had he done but very cleverly put her at fault? Furthermore, he had refused responsibility for Randolph's predicament, and she could not let him get away with that!

"Captain Hillary," she said stiffly, holding herself very straight, as though somehow, despite her red curls and that charming retroussé nose, she could look severe. "I know that my cousin has been enlisted to collect information for you, information about his own father as a magistrate and about the criminal activity in the town. I know, as well, that you took him on not because he has any experience in these matters or has worked for a newspaper before, but because he could tell you things about his father which might be helpful."

"You make me sound singularly offensive, Miss Eaton," he said, and his voice was grim.

"I expect you are someone to be feared," Alicia told him, unable now to stop herself. "Something about you tells me that you are single-minded, that you will let nothing stand in your way. I expect—I expect that you only know how to make use of people. In the war you used your soldiers and now you are using Randolph. . . ."

"Soon you will be saying that I sought you out to speak to you for a particular purpose, Miss Eaton," he murmured.

Alicia was aware that they were making something of a sensation. People knew who the captain was. Bath was too small a place for that to have been prevented. They must also know that he planned to make *The Gazette* into an organ of reform, which told them something about his character. As for his appearance, that was so clearly different, even down to the black satin of his coat and pantaloons, which he wore in such a way as to make the other gentlemen in the room look like so many peacocks in their pastel silks and satins. Add to all this the fact that nothing could be clearer than that he and Alicia were having something which did not fall far short of an altercation, and it was only natural that they should have attracted stares. Indeed, even the young viscount with whom Alicia had been dancing paused at a distance with two glasses of punch in his hands, apparently deciding not to interrupt.

"Well, sir," Alicia was replying, "I think it very unlikely that, on the basis of one meeting during which you scarcely looked at me, you developed a single-minded yearning to talk to me on this particular night."

"Your tongue is sharper than I had imagined," he told her.

"You do not bring out my better nature, Captain," Alicia told him frankly. "Not that I think a sharp tongue will help me, for I see that you mean to make no apology for having led Randolph on."

She wished he would not look at her so steadily. She hoped he would not see she minded. She wanted to turn away and leave him and somehow found she could not do it.

"As a matter of fact," he said quite coolly, "I was looking for your cousin."

She had been right about him then, Alicia thought. The only reason he had spoken to her was because he wanted some information. Very well! But she was not about to help him. As a matter of fact Randolph was in a side room, playing whist.

"If I were to ask you what he was wanted for, you would not tell me, I suppose?" she murmured.

"Is he here?" Captain Hillary said flatly.

How Alicia hated being condescended to in this way. It would have been something had he simply said that no, he would not tell her, that there were reasons why secrecy must be maintained. Even if he lied in saying something of that manner, she would not feel this way. It was an insult for him to avoid her questions in this matter. To simply disregard them as though she had not spoken! Oh, if only she were a gentleman, she would call him out!

But because she was a lady and could not take action, she lied instead.

"As a matter of fact," she told him. "If you came here to find Randolph, you must be disappointed. He and Mr. Soupcon are across the river at the pleasure gardens, it being such a fine night. There is such a crowd there, I believe, and the boats so hard to hire, not to mention the lateness of the evening, that I expect he will be difficult to . . ."

She broke off, aware that the captain was staring at someone over her shoulder. And when she turned, she saw that someone was Randolph with young Soupcon beside him, and that they were talking and laughing in their usual lighthearted way. Looking back at the captain, she met grim eyes.

"Did it give you pleasure to mock me, Miss Eaton?" he demanded.

"The less you see of my cousin, the better it will be for both of them, sir," Alicia replied. "I wish that you would listen to me, although I expect you are too proud to do it. If you can have no pity for Randolph, no sense of guilt about using him because of his father, at least you should consider that he is feckless. He will make mistakes which, at the very least, you will find troublesome. He is my cousin and I am fond of him, but I must warn you that he is not to be depended on for long. He may feel just at present that he is playing an exciting game. But he will soon grow tired of it, or make such an effort as to put himself, and perhaps you, in danger."

The captain laughed then, and Alicia thought that worse than his anger. "In other words, Miss Eaton, you have dispatched all your arrows. You have appealed to me as a gentleman, made certain threats, and now you warn me that your cousin may put me in danger. Now it is my turn to assure you of two things. That is, if you will permit it."

Alicia's polonaise gown was a soft blue, sprigged with white, and it had occurred to her this evening as she had seen herself in the pier glass in her bedchamber that she looked more demure than she would like. It had been the oddest fancy, for the dress had been made by her mother particularly for occasions like this, and she had never found fault with it before. Now once again she found herself wishing that she did not look quite such a girl. How could she expect the captain to take anything she said seriously enough? But before she could make any response, Randolph and young Soupcon had joined them, their smiles and laughter fading as they saw the captain.

He bowed and asked her to excuse him. As soon as he had retired with her cousin and his friend, Imogene joined her, like someone who has been waiting in the wings.

"What on earth were you saying to him?" she demanded. "Why, I declare, for a while I thought that he was in a fury! What a dangerous gentleman he looks sometimes. I expect it is his darkness and . . . Oh, Alicia, why do you let me go on babbling? Did he tell you what Randolph is doing for him? Did he let slip any details . . ."

Alicia did not answer. Captain Hillary was leading her cousin and young Soupcon out of the room. Not a few young ladies looked regretful, and Alicia knew it was not Randolph's departing which distressed them. Captain Hillary must seem a prize, since he was rich and handsome and mysterious as well. But she knew better. He was, she thought, the most contemptible man she had ever met.

"I tried to make my way through the crowd to join you while you were still in conversation with the dear captain!" Lady Fairbreaks exclaimed, appearing breathless at Alicia's side. "It would have been the perfect opportunity for me to have invited him to us for an entertainment. I do not care what your father says, Imogene. I mean to have the captain as my guest. And now it seems that he and Randolph know one another! How very thrilling!"

"I think we must find out precisely what it is my brother is doing," Imogene said in a low voice as her mother rambled on.

"And I am in agreement," Alicia told her in a determined way. "Even if it means that certain risks are taken, we must put ourselves in the captain's way."

CHAPTER SEVEN

The next day the two girls excused themselves from accompanying Lady Fairbreaks to the Pump Room and proceeded to make their plans. From the direction of Sir Humphrey's offices, his angry voice could be heard rising and falling as he berated miscreants right and left. *The Gazette* had become increasingly insistent of late that considerable numbers of crimes within the city went undetected and, if detected, unpunished. Every day Sir Humphrey became grimmer. What he would say when he discovered that his own son was working to help the gentleman who was writing these stories, Alicia did not care to think. She only hoped that she and Imogene could somehow manage to discover enough about what Randolph was doing to be able to dissuade him before he was found out.

It was agreed after considerable discussion that since, except for the night before, when Randolph had gone to the Assembly Rooms, he had formed the habit of leaving the house at about the time they set out on their expedition to some soirée or other, and he was not to be seen again until the morning.

"Clearly we must arrange to follow him," Imogene declared. "But since Mama expects us to accompany her every evening, I do not know how it can be arranged."

For a long while they sat in silence in the sunny parlor, with Sir Humphrey's bellow sounding occasionally from the further side of the house.

"We could both pretend to have megrims," Imogene said hopefully at last.

Alicia suggested that not only was the coincidence of simultaneous headaches unlikely but that it might well happen that Lady Fairbreaks would decide to stay home and nurse them. Another silence followed, this one deeper than before.

"Tonight we are to attend the concert," Alicia said finally. "Your mother has arranged to have the carriage pick up Mrs. Tanner on the half hour before it begins. Now, this is what I think that we should do."

Lady Fairbreaks was a creature of habit. Furthermore, she had a dread of being late for any entertainment. Add to this the fact that she liked to maintain the fiction that delays and accidents and things unplanned for in general only happened to her friends, never to herself. All this Alicia had taken into her calculation, and thus it was that when they were just on the brink of leaving the house that evening and Alicia discovered that the hem of her gown was torn, it seemed only natural that Lady Fairbreaks should go on in the carriage to pick up Mrs. Tanner and proceed to the concert hall accordingly. Meanwhile, the two girls could be trusted to walk the short distance to their destination, particularly as it was not yet dusk. As for seating arrangements, Alicia and Imogene were particularly assiduous in urging Lady Fairbreaks to see that she and Mrs. Tanner took the best seats that they could. As for the girls, they would sit anywhere they could find room, meeting Lady Fairbreaks and her companion in the foyer when the concert was over.

It was a simple plan and worked accordingly. The torn hem, coming as a surprise, did not allow Lady Fairbreaks an opportunity to consider the ins and outs of the arrangement, particularly since the girls came up so quickly with alternative arrangements. Within minutes she was bundled into the carriage, resplendent in her florid manner in a green silk gown with a low-cut square bodice, with her powdered hair piled very high and decorated with three languid feathers. Waving her out of sight, the two girls hurried back into the house and secreted themselves in a second sitting room, which was rarely used but which had the advantage of a window that looked out onto the street.

Not long after Lady Fairbreaks's carriage had disappeared down the narrow street, Randolph's steps were heard on the stairs, and soon he appeared on the doorstep, where he paused to look around him. Alicia and Imogene both held their breath. From the next room the faint sounds of Sir Humphrey snoring could be heard. Alicia just had time to think how much of the time her uncle made his presence known in just that way, raised voice or snore, but always from another room, before Randolph hurried down the steps into the street and started off in the direction of the North Parade.

Although the evening promised to be mild, both girls had provided themselves with hooded capes of a dark shade of gray. Pulling them over their shoulders, they hurried to follow Randolph, who with his usual bland confidence apparently entertained no fears that he was being followed.

"After all, if he does see us, what can he do or say?" Imogene had said when they had first conceived their plan. "If he is angry, well, I will only shrug my shoulders and tell him that we will try again another day."

Now, however, in the actual moments, both girls were more subdued, particularly when Randolph turned aside from the North Parade, which at this hour of the evening was filled with carriages and people on foot making their way to a variety of entertainments. And when he turned into an alley, Alicia felt Imogene clutch her arm.

"Rats!" her cousin whispered. "I am terrified by rats! They come up from the river every evening and lurk about in places like that."

There had been a time, Alicia knew, not many days ago at that, when she would have welcomed the excuse to abandon what she then would have referred to as a reckless endeavor. Now, however, following her encounter with the captain, she was so committed to somehow breaking the line between him and her cousin that she tugged Imogene ahead impatiently.

"I will walk first," she told her, "and if there are rats about, they will run off. Try not to think of it, and come along before we lose sight of him completely."

Imogene did what she was told, albeit reluctantly, and they reached the entrance to the alley in time to see Randolph reach the end of it and turn right. There was no need for Alicia to tell her cousin to hurry. Thoughts of lurking rats were quite enough to cause Imogene to break into a run with her cape billowing around her. So swift were they that they were in time to see Randolph enter a building not a hundred yards from where they were standing, an abandoned building with broken windows and a general air of neglect.

"Well, he has not come far from home," Alicia said in a whisper. "Still, it is quite another sort of neighborhood. I think we can be sure enough what his business is about."

"Do you expect he meets with criminals?" Imogene demanded. "I mean to say, what are we to do now? Shall we go home? Go along to the concert? La, I cannot think now what we are about!"

"We have come this far and we must continue," Alicia said in the same voice she reserved for her father's curate, a highly nervous fellow who tended to panic when required to address the congregation.

"Do you mean we are to go up and knock on the door?" Imogene said nervously. "Why, Alicia, that would be madness! They would take us inside and tie us to chairs! Hold us hostage! Force us to undergo . . ."

Alicia had never guessed that her cousin possessed quite such a fevered imagination, and suspected that she might have been conditioned, if only indirectly, by her father's daily association with the criminal class.

"You forget that whoever is inside there, your brother is with them," Alicia said, knowing it was not the most reassuring argument but using it as the only one she had. "Besides, I do not mean to have us take chances. We only need to find a way to hear something of what is going on."

They had remained in the shelter of the alley as they spoke, and it occurred to Alicia that no doubt there was another space very like this beside the house her cousin had entered. At all events it would do no harm to see. There was no light at the front of the building, and it stood to reason, consequently, that if there was a meeting of some sort, it was going on at the back.

There was some problem in convincing Imogene that this was what they should do, but Alicia, once started on a project, was difficult to resist. Finally they slipped across the street like two gray shadows and found that there was, indeed, another alley very like the first.

It was becoming truly dark now, which fact filled Imogene with so much anxiety that Alicia had to push and pull her along. And suddenly they were in a little garden, or a plot of land that once had been one. Roses, growing wild, thrust out their thorns, and their odor mingled with another which was dank and vaguely unpleasant.

"La, I do not like it here!" Imogene whispered. "Let us go back home, Alicia, please. Randolph is of an age to get himself out of any difficulty. Besides, I am certain that Captain Hillary would not let him put himself in danger. I was wrong to be concerned. I was . . ."

Alicia pressed her finger to her cousin's lips and pointed at a window just above their heads. A flickering light was shining from it, and there was a sound of voices, one of which Alicia thought she recognized as her cousin's.

"What I want to know, sir," a man's voice suddenly declared, surprisingly clear due to a combination of cracked glass and the fact that, apparently, he had moved near the window, "is how you knew that I was to come down from London and begin my operation in Bath."

Alicia was certain that it was Randolph who answered him, and she knew from the way Imogene pressed her arm excitedly that she thought so, too. It was not clear precisely what he was saying, however, perhaps because he was standing on the other side of the room.

"You must understand," a third voice announced, shrill and strangely pitched, with more than a hint of the "wrong" accent to it, "that Lord Tommy wants to come and go without his business being reported in a gazette. Whoever this Captain Hillary is, you want to tell him that."

Apparently this remark inspired Randolph to make a joke, for he sounded mightily amused and followed his remark with laughter. Alicia wondered if he realized that he was laughing alone.

"The chap's a fool, sir," they heard the third man say while Randolph was still enjoying his little witticism.

"All of which could make him more dangerous," the man who had spoken first explained. "I'd give a good deal to know where he got his information about what we are planning here at Bath."

"It's my opinion he don't know much, sir, and that's a fact. Give him a good scare and let him go is my opinion."

At that they seemed to move away from the window, and their words became unintelligible. "Let's hurry away now!" Imogene whispered, clearly in a panic. "They don't intend to really hurt him, and a scare never does anyone any harm!"

This expression of sisterly devotion did not come as a surprise to Alicia. It had been clear to her from the moment she had come to Bath that life in her uncle's household meant every man for himself.

"I want to know everything that happens," she said now, resisting Imogene and her tuggings. "I intend to tell Captain Hillary that I have proof that because of him Randolph is being put in danger. And I want you as my witness.

It was not absolutely clear to Alicia what her motive was. Of course she wanted to protect her cousin. But she also knew that it would give her great pleasure to be able to demonstrate to the captain that he had been mistaken in condescending to her, to have made it so clear that her opinion did not matter.

At the same moment that this thought passed through her mind, she noted in the growing darkness a low construction built to the right of the window, which had served, no doubt, in the days of the structure's prosperity, as some sort of storage area. Furthermore, some crates were piled beside it. But when Alicia signified her intention, Imogene absolutely refused. It would serve no purpose, she whispered in a frantic way. And since this was neither the time nor place for Alicia to explain that, on the contrary, it would serve a considerable purpose indeed, she said that if she could not have Imogene as witness, she would be obliged to tell her father about tonight's activities, knowing that it would give Sir Humphrey precisely the edge he needed over his saucy daughter, something he could use to keep her in control forever.

It was with obvious reluctance that Imogene then followed, but at least she was as graceful and as silent as was Alicia, whose training for such escapades went back to childhood exploits concerning the climbing of walls, exploits which seemed now, in memory, to have filled up one sunlit day after another until the time had come for her to put on long skirts forever and learn to be a lady.

But she did not feel like a lady tonight—only an adventurer. Drawing Imogene after her, she edged her way along the flat roof of the shed until they were close beside the window and able to look, at last, into the room.

They saw a shabby room with cracked walls, a bare and dirty floor, and no furniture. A single candle burned in a holder on the window ledge, throwing great shadows into the room. Randolph was standing backed against the door, and the two gentlemen the girls had overheard were talking to him earnestly. One of them was short and reminded Alicia, somehow, of a smooth gray stone. Everything about him seemed gently rounded, from his smooth powdered hair to his round cheeks, down to his rotund form. And yet there was something about his heavy-lidded eyes which was ominous, foreboding. She could easily see him edging around corners, forever in a shadow.

As for the other man, he caught Alicia's full attention, for she was certain that he must be Lord Tommy. Tall and handsome, he had fair hair powdered and arranged as elegantly as though he were in the smartest house in London. His coat and waistcoat were of canary yellow and beautifully embroidered, and he wore matching pantaloons. When Imogene took a wrong step and sent some roofing clattering down into the garden, he was the first one to come to the broken window and throw up the sash.

"Well, what is this?" he inquired politely, picking up the candle by its holder and raising it to see their faces. "Two young ladies climbing about at the back of deserted buildings in the night! In London that would be thought a bit unusual, but no doubt in Bath it is the latest fashion, although why anyone would want to do it I cannot imagine."

"Alicia!" Randolph cried, having hurried to the window. "Imogene!"

"Ah, they are your familiars," the man Alicia took to be Sir Tommy said with a faint smile. "Well, in that case, ladies, you must enter. Brad and I will help you through the window. Yes. Just so. It would be extremely silly not to accept the invitation. Allow me to introduce myself and my companion. I am Lord Taavis, and this is Mr. Bradshaw. There is no need to be put off by his appearance. And now, perhaps one of you will tell me how it happened that you were eavesdropping on a very private conversation."

CHAPTER EIGHT

The next morning the events of the night before seemed to Alicia to be like a dream of a rather unpleasant nature, not, in fact, a nightmare but something in between. It was necessary for her to hurry down to breakfast if for no other reason than to indicate that nothing out of the way had happened, for above all, she did not want to attract attention. But what she found she wanted more than anything was to get her thoughts in order. The night before, she had meant to do it, but when the excitement had died down at last and she had been safely in her bedchamber, sleep had claimed her before she had even guessed at its approach.

Now, however, as she entered the breakfast room, it became apparent that the atmosphere was not conducive to quiet thought. Sir Humphrey sat at one end of the table, wearing his black horsehair wig and a furious expression, while facing him at a safe distance and apparently quite calm, Lady Fairbreaks was describing a wall mirror she had decided to buy. It seemed an innocent enough subject to Alicia, but clearly something about it had put her uncle out of temper.

"This particular piece comes from the glassworks of the Duke of Buckingham himself," Lady Fairbreaks continued calmly, including Alicia in the conversation with a nod. "I declare that it is clearer than any glass I have ever seen coming from Venice, and the piece I have in mind is convex, as well, which I always find amusing."

"The cost, madam, the cost!" Alicia heard her uncle mutter from between clenched teeth. "You will make a poor man of me in the end. If only I did not have troubles enough presently without you talking of convex glass!"

For all the attention that Lady Fairbreaks gave him, he might as well not have spoken. "Such a pretty piece," she told Alicia. "Just what is needed for the hall. There is a great deal of gilding about it. Quite an elaborate pattern indeed, which is, of course, what makes it so expensive. Why, did you know that the dealer told me that gilding is one of the more highly paid trades. In fact a gilder makes a penny more in an hour than a wood-carver, if you can believe it. He explained it all quite carefully to me, to justify the price."

"The price, madam!" Sir Humphrey shouted, pounding the table hard enough to rattle his wife's cup in its saucer. "I am the one who has to pay it! Why, damme, you will spend me out of house and home!"

"You must not mind your uncle, dear," Lady

Fairbreaks said to Alicia, smiling in her florid way. "He is always out of temper lately over one thing or another. He will rail at anything, I think. Sit down and have a cup of tea and some bread and butter. And there is some lovely jelly which Mrs. Tanner's cook made up herself. Dear Dorine was so sorry not to see you or Imogene last night at the concert, but it was only understandable that we should not have met you, considering the crush. And it all worked out quite nicely, since you met Randolph and his friends and came home in their carriage. Fancy Randolph going to a concert! What did you girls tell me the names of his friends are? I declare it has quite slipped my mind."

At the other end of the table, Sir Humphrey had subsided into a fit of grumbling which did not prevent him from making a substantial breakfast consisting of steak and ale, which once the little maid set it before him, he turned to with gusto.

"One gentleman is Lord Taavis, Mama," Imogene declared, having overheard the question as she entered the breakfast room. "And the other is a Mr. Bradshaw."

For a moment the two girls met one another's eyes. There had been no time the evening before for them to agree on how much they should or should not say.

"And one of them you find attractive," Lady Fairbreaks said archly. "Don't tell me no, my dear. I saw the way you looked last night. I pride myself on knowing all the symptoms when a gel's in love."

"Mama!" Imogene declared in a disgusted way. But her color heightened, and remembering the events of the night before, Alicia thought, to her dismay, that Lady Fairbreaks might be correct in her diagnosis.

It had been an awkward moment when they had all stood there together in that dusty room with the candle throwing their shadows onto the damp and peeling walls. Randolph had begun to sputter, but before he could say too little or too much, Lord Taavis had pursued his line of questioning, hoping, no doubt, to find one that could be answered easily, one that would set them off on their explanations.

"Are you perhaps this gentleman's confederates?" he asked in the most charming way, his blue eyes lingering on Alicia with a certain appreciation which she could not mistake. "Are you being paid by the captain to spy on me? Hillary's reputation had led me to expect him to take a more subtle course, I must confess. But if he will hire boys and ladies . . ."

"I am not a boy, sir!" Randolph exclaimed, clearly deeply stung by the remark.

"And we do not work for Captain Hillary!" Imogene had told him.

"You ought to know right now you can't play Lord Tommy for a fool, miss," the second man said in a belligerent way. "We know what Hillary is up to well enough."

"Well, if you do that is more than we can say," Alicia had said, putting her arm about Imogene. "We came here because . . ."

"Why should the captain be interested in you, sir?" Imogene interrupted her. Even in the insufficient light it was evident that she was in an excited state which had nothing to do with fear or nervousness. That had been the moment when Alicia had first guessed that her cousin found this tall, fair man whom his companion called Lord Tommy something more than the passing stranger who had been met in the most unusual of circumstances.

Lord Taavis seemed more amused than anything, although Mr. Bradshaw clearly bridled at the question and Randolph shot his sister an appealing glance.

"Well, Miss Fairbreaks," Lord Tommy Taavis had replied, "I will make you a bargain."

"He can't resist a gamble, Lord Tommy can't," Mr. Bradshaw said as though he was talking to himself.

"I will agree to tell you what you want to know," his companion continued, "if you will tell me what you are doing here. And one thing more."

"He always pads his bets," Mr. Bradshaw was heard to observe, although no one took any notice.

"And that is, sir?" Alicia said quite sharply.

"I will expect the promise of both of you to

save me a dance at the next Assembly Rooms ball."

Alicia did not like the way he was smiling at her. Indeed, underneath his charm and his good humor, she sensed something very dangerous indeed. The sooner they could be out of this deserted house the better, she decided. But Imogene, for her own reasons, had already agreed before Alicia could say a word.

"They must have followed me for some reason," Randolph muttered. The events of the evening had clearly put him in a distracted state of mind. Indeed, despite his powdered hair and foppish clothes, he looked more like a boy than Alicia could have believed possible.

"We wanted to protect you," Imogene declared. "We thought you were involved with some dangerous characters, some people connected with crime in Bath. We never imagined that we would find you with someone like—like Lord Taavis."

"Someone so eminently respectable, you mean?" the gentleman she referred to said in a mocking way. "You notice that Miss Fairbreaks did not include you, Brad, good fellow! What ho! I had not expected this evening to turn into a lark! So my appearance has reassured you, my dear young lady."

There was a familiarity in the way he spoke to Imogene which displeased Alicia, and when Lord Taavis turned to her, she gave him notice with her eyes that he should stay closer to the mark.

"I have annoyed you, Miss Eaton," he said with a little bow. "Indeed, I am sorry for it. Permit me to assure you that you will be driven home in my carriage, which Brad and I thought practical to leave a bit out of the way. I mean to say that you will be treated with every indication of respect."

"Then let us bring this encounter to a close as quickly as possible, sir," Alicia said sharply.

"You mean to join Miss Fairbreaks in making a bargain with me, then?" he asked her, a smile lingering on his lips, a smile which seemed to make him more dangerous still.

Alicia considered. A dance was nothing. And Imogene had already blurted out their reason for being here. Besides, the more information she could present to Captain Hillary to indicate that he was placing Randolph in danger, the better.

"You may have your dance, sir, if you want it," Alicia replied. "My cousin has told you our reason for being here. And now, if you will honor your part of the bargain and tell us how it is that Captain Hillary should be interested in your doings, we can take our leave of one another."

"That is a moment I would not like to hasten, Miss Eaton," Lord Taavis assured her. "However, I can tell you briefly that I am what is known as a gentleman scoundrel. That is to say, I take my particular pleasure at the gaming tables. I am an intimate of every faro bank held along Pall Mall in London. If it were not for my rank, no doubt I would be called a sharpster. I have come to Bath to set up a private club, in a manner of speaking. To put it plainly to you charming young ladies, I like to relieve wealthy gentlemen of their purses. All quite fair and square, I assure you. We play. I win. That is the way of it. And if Brad here is not precisely my right hand, he is as good a left as any I have ever known."

It had been plain speaking. Even Alicia had not been able to fault it. But before either she or Imogene could make reply, Lord Taavis had continued on a less casual note.

"When you two young ladies made your unexpected appearance, I was about to tell this gentleman the purpose I had in setting up this appointment. Your brother has become something of a nuisance, Miss Fairbreaks. I can see that you understand me. Brad and I are busy setting up our operation, and your brother is constantly underfoot. That was why we set up this meeting. We wanted to tell him that we were displeased."

"You meant to threaten him," Alicia had declared with conviction.

"Why, as for that, if you had not joined us, Miss Eaton, we might have more than threatened," Lord Taavis said in his charming way.

"It would have been no more than Randolph deserved, I'm sure," Imogene said in her usual sympathetic manner. "I know you would not have hurt him badly."

From the expression in Randolph's eyes, Alicia thought that was a point about which he was not so certain.

"I think what we will do now, however," Lord Taavis went on pleasantly, "is to send a message to Captain Hillary that I do not wish to see my name appearing in his newspaper and that if I do see it featured there, I will take the proper steps. Will you tell him that for me, Mr. Fairbreaks?"

"I will be glad to tell him," Alicia said before her cousin could answer.

"What's that, eh? I thought you had nothing to do with this business, miss," Mr. Bradshaw said in a rough manner.

Lord Taavis gave him a warning look. "I expect Miss Eaton has her own reasons," he said. "Actually, I would be delighted if she would do precisely that. I have heard that Captain Hillary does not allow his head to be turned by ladies, but all the same, given your beauty, Miss Eaton . . ."

"My appearance has nothing to do with anything," Alicia told him, wavering between losing her temper and being sensible enough to control it. "I have my own private reasons for wanting the captain to be aware that he cannot manipulate people."

She had cut herself off then, knowing that she had said more than she should already. The terms of the bargain having been fulfilled, they had left the building by the back and found a carriage waiting on a side street, and a liveried driver with it. Despite her repeated objections that she and her cousins could quite easily walk wherever they were going, Lord Taavis had insisted that they be driven home in style. Furthermore, on parting, Imogene had allowed him to kiss her hand in the Continental fashion, while Alicia went straight on into the house.

Once the three young people were inside together and Lord Taavis and Mr. Bradshaw had driven away, there was no opportunity for them to talk together, even though it was clear that there was a great deal to say. Alicia had only had time to note how pale Randolph was looking and observe the glitter in Imogene's eyes when Lady Fairbreaks had come fussing in from the concert, expressing a passionate relief that they had got home safely. As far as she was concerned, they had spent a musical evening, and in silent agreement, they had not attempted to make any other explanation than that they had been brought home by two of Randolph's friends, which was, with the exception of a single word, the truth.

Alicia had hoped that Lady Fairbreaks would forget that part of the evening completely, and no doubt she would have done had she not been astute enough to sense that her daughter had been unduly impressed by one of the gentlemen her brother had "introduced" her to. Alicia realized that Lady Fairbreaks was just now declaring that she must meet the gentleman. And, of course, his friend, as well. Imogene looked delighted, although, Alicia noted, Randolph blanched.

"La, I will invite them to the little entertainment I am holding at the beginning of the week," Lady Fairbreaks declared. "I am inviting that interesting Captain Hillary as well, you know, just as I promised, for I must persuade him that the social news should be expanded, rather than the other way. On the whole, people have no desire to read on and on about reform and crime and all that boring nonsense."

Given the fact that Lady Fairbreaks's husband was a magistrate, it came as no surprise to Alicia that he should raise his head at that, much in the manner of an enraged bull.

"Nonsense, madam!" he declared. "Damme, that is just what that Hillary would like to hear any wife of mine say! And as for inviting him, I hope you do not mean here to this house!"

"Wherever else could I invite him, sir?" Lady Fairbreaks said with a little laugh, as though her husband were trying, unsuccessfully, to be amusing.

"Damme!" Sir Humphrey cried for a second time, starting to his feet. "If you have the man here, I will not receive him. And as for this Lord Taavis you were speaking of, he is a great scoundrel and maybe worse! I had heard that he was down from London and had taken a house in the Royal Crescent, but I never expected to hear my own wife . . ."

But Alicia did not hear the rest of what her uncle had to say, for Imogene, with her usual regard for her parents, leaned across the narrow table, beaming.

"Oh, dear!" she said. "I knew it was fated from the first moment I laid eyes on him, Alicia! And

95

now I can be quite certain that we were meant for one another. Only fancy, he has taken a house on the Royal Crescent! You heard what I said the other day. I do not care if he is a scoundrel. They are as good as other people, I dare say. But there! We will talk about it later. Just now, since Papa is in a temper, I suppose we should listen to whatever it is he is trying to say."

CHAPTER NINE

Whatever it was that Sir Humphrey finally said, it was completely disregarded by Lady Fairbreaks, who proceeded to plan her party with all the energy that she could muster. Indeed, she began immediately that morning, as soon as Sir Humphrey had stormed off to his offices to hear the cases for the day. Imogene's help was enlisted, and an attempt was made to take advantage of every one of Alicia's waking hours as well, but she pleaded special business of her own which would take her all the morning.

Lady Fairbreaks, fortunately, was too interested in her own plans to be curious and went off with Imogene, who had turned quite docile at the thought of having Lord Tommy Taavis under her roof. Alicia was just about to leave the breakfast room when Randolph made his appearance, and since they were alone and it was safe enough to talk, she asked him what he meant to do after last night's misadventure.

Randolph, it soon appeared, had, in his usual careless fashion, been able to sleep off any terror which had struck him the night before. Lord Taavis was a gentleman, he told her, although what assurance that was to him, Alicia did not know. Besides, Randolph went on to tell her, when Lord Taavis understood clearly what was wanted of him, he would make no objection.

"'Pon my soul, I tried to make an explanation," her cousin told her. "Tried to make it clear just what I was scouting about him for. But in the end he wouldn't listen, and then you and Imogene came along."

Alicia eyed him speculatively. Could he possibly believe that he would not be in danger if he pursued his present course? All the more reason for her to persuade Captain Hillary of the need to dispense with her cousin's services at once.

"Just what do you have in mind?" she asked him, straightening her white mobcap on her red curls. "I mean to say, surely you intended to observe his gaming activities and make a report of them to—to the captain."

"Oh, I am far more clever than that!" Randolph assured her with a cheerful smile. "Lord Tommy means a faro bank here in Bath, and I do not know what else besides. Now, what sort of people will that attract?"

"People who wish to be separated from their money as soon as possible, I expect," Alicia said pertly.

"There is more to it than that," her cousin told her, settling his long, narrow person in a chair and stretching out his legs as he took up a bun and began to munch it. "Everyone knows that serious gambling such as he has in mind attracts the underworld. Why, every petty criminal in Bath will come out from under a stone. Lord Tommy will not have been a week in town when he will know everyone who should be prosecuted."

"What has that to do with you?" Alicia asked him impatiently. There was something about Randolph's ways which were an irritation to her. Even his quizzing glass, which was hanging from a gold chain, offended her this morning, and for a moment she wondered if the general mood most prevalent in this household was catching like the pox.

"Why, I intend to persuade Lord Tommy to give me information," her cousin told her blandly. "Then we will know just who is doing what, when, and where. Those are key words in journalism, you know, and I think there is another, although I have forgot it."

"And just what will Lord Taavis receive in return for all this information?" Alicia asked him dryly. "Or is he to do it out of friendship. Somehow, after the way he behaved to you last night, I do not think that he entirely understands the situation."

"Why, I'll be a gammon if he won't appreciate the opportunity to give me information," her cousin told her, picking an apple out of the bowl in the center of the table. "As for what I will give him in return, it's to be journalistic protection.

Captain Hillary will agree not to mention his name in print."

Alicia stared at him in a disbelieving way. "Have you Captain Hillary's word on this?" she demanded. "Has he really agreed to such an arrangement?"

"Well, as for that, I have not mentioned the matter to him in precisely that way," Randolph told her, taking a large bite of the apple. "But I mean to later today. Or perhaps I will simply make Lord Tommy the promise and then . . ."

"Hope for the best?" Alicia demanded. "Randolph, you cannot be such a fool as that! Captain Hillary is certain to find out about Lord Taavis's activities, whether you tell him or not. And if he thinks there is a danger that a faro bank is to be established, he will write editorials about it. And then, I ask you, where will you be? Even assuming that Lord Taavis would make the agreement you propose—which I do not think is in the least certain—he would have the right to expect it to be upheld. On the occasion of the first editorial against him . . ."

"Ladies never understand business matters," Randolph told her. "I can understand that you were probably frightened by Lord Tommy and his friend last evening, but I assure you . . ."

"I assure *you* that they both are dangerous!" Alicia told him. "But that is something that, clearly, *you* cannot understand."

And with that she whirled out of the breakfast room, leaving Randolph staring after her. In a matter of minutes she was arrayed in a morning gown of pale blue silk with a gauze neckerchief arranged in a modest way, and a dormeuse covering her red curls. She knew that *The Gazette* offices were on the first right turning off York Street, and it was in this direction that she briskly made her way, avoiding the crowds about the Pump Room by taking side streets, where after an early morning rain, the cobbles glittered in the sunlight and landladies opened their windows wide to the fresh breezes which blew in from the river.

Reaching the door of the newspaper office, Alicia drew herself up very straight. Try as she would not to, she dreaded this encounter. First of all, she must not allow herself to lose her temper. If she did, Captain Hillary would take advantage of her in a flash. Her father had always told her that the reasoned argument counted most. And so, no matter how condescendingly the captain treated her, she would make a case based on logic, a case which he could not refute in any way. To reinforce her determination, she remembered the particular way Lord Taavis had smiled and the smooth, gray overtones of Mr. Bradshaw.

The door opened into a narrow corridor from which she could hear the presses being run. Opening the first door on her right, Alicia found herself in an office where, behind a desk piled with papers, Captain Hillary sat.

He should have been less imposing than when she had seen him last, for he wore no coat or cravat and his lawn shirt was open at the neck, his sleeves rolled back nearly to the elbows. His dark hair was unpowdered and pulled back in a queue, giving a certain severity to his dark-skinned, handsome face which Alicia had not seen before.

Clearly he was amazed to see her. And yet he rose slowly and made his bow with reserve. "Miss Eaton," he said in a low voice. "To what do I owe this honor?"

"I do not know whether you will consider it an honor when I have finished, sir," Alicia said in what she hoped was a most businesslike way.

"Well, then, pray be seated, and we will see," he told her, indicating a chair. "I assume it is some social notice which you wish to have included in a column. Perhaps a mention of the soirée which your aunt is holding. I have just received the invitation."

How easily he could enrage her, Alicia thought, although, in all fairness, he probably had not meant to do so in this case. A social notice, indeed! Did he think all she had to occupy her mind was that sort of business? Well, she would prove to him that he was mistaken!

"I am not concerned with social notices, sir," she replied, keeping her voice even with an effort. "If my aunt has invited you to some function or other, it is no concern of mine."

That sounded ungracious, she realized, but that was just as it should be. She had not come here, after all, to exchange pleasantries with him. And she did not want him to think, not for an instant, that he had been invited on her account.

For a moment she thought of asking him if he had accepted, but then decided against it. If she asked, he would, no doubt, compliment himself by thinking that she was looking forward to seeing him in a social situation.

"Well then, Miss Eaton," he responded, "what, precisely, can I do for you?"

He did not add that this was a busy office, but the implication was certainly there, she thought. She could hear the slap-slap of the paper going through the press and realized that she would have been interested if he had asked her to see the operation in motion, in a way of speaking. But of course he was only eager for her to state her business and be gone. And of course she was more than eager to oblige him. The sooner she left this office, the better, even though there was something about it which appealed . . .

But no matter. She must state her case, convince him, and return to the house on the North Parade. At noon there would be the abbey and afterward a heavy dinner and the preparations for the ball at the Assembly Hall. How odd it was that the routine should seem, just at this moment, to be so monotonous.

"I have come on account of my cousin Randolph," she told him. "Because of his contact with a certain Lord Taavis. Do you know the man I mean?"

"Taavis!" Captain Hillary exclaimed, and she had the pleasure of seeing him surprised. "What could your cousin possibly have to do with that scoundrel, since he makes his base in London."

"That is precisely the way he likes to hear himself described," Alicia said quickly. "The gentleman scoundrel" is the precise term, I believe, that he prefers."

The captain, who had remained standing, leaned on his desk and stared at her so closely that she prayed she would not blush.

"What would you know of someone like Lord Taavis?" he demanded. "Certainly you cannot have met him."

"I had that very pleasure," Alicia assured him. "Last night he and a friend of his, a Mr. Bradshaw, had arranged a secret meeting with my cousin Randolph."

"What! Here in Bath?"

Alicia felt a mounting excitement. She *had* taken him by surprise, then. The great newspaper man was listening to her seriously, at last. She could not resist the chance to delay her disclosures. She would make him dig for them. After all, it was no more than he deserved after his treatment of her the other evening at the Assembly Rooms.

"I have not been in any other place for the past two weeks, sir," she replied.

"Do not be demure, Miss Eaton. It does not suit you."

The remark took her so much by surprise that for a moment she could not answer him. Then she rallied her self-possession and said, "I saw him last night. Mr. Bradshaw was with him. They were meeting with Randolph."

"Meeting?" His eyes were like steel in the way they held hers. "And where was this, Miss Eaton?"

"In a deserted house somewhere off the North Parade," she told him, keeping her face as expressionless as possible, as though she was accustomed to this sort of discussion, as though it did not shock her and therefore should not shock him, as well.

"A deserted house! And you were there?"

"With my cousin, Miss Fairbreaks."

"And Randolph took you! I cannot believe what I am hearing. Why, I knew that he was a fool but . . ."

"I hoped to hear you say that," Alicia told him. "It is all the proof I need that you were determined to take advantage of him. Well, sir, now this 'fool' has stumbled onto an idea which has already put him in considerable danger. And because he cannot see it, he is making plans which will practically ensure that something will happen to him. I have come here to demand that you prevent it."

She had gone about it the right way. His attention was engaged, and he was outraged. Why was it that she did not feel more triumphant? She watched Captain Hillary walk around the desk. She did not avoid his eyes. There seemed to be accusation in them, although, of course, that was absurd.

Captain Hillary stopped before her. He was wearing riding breeches and boots, and that, combined with the effect of the lawn shirt, open necked as it was, managed to convey an essence of masculinity which was so strong that Alicia felt disturbed. Her father was never to be seen without the neat costume of his office as vicar, her uncle and the other gentlemen she knew dressed all the time in silk and satin, but there was something here which was quite different. She was aware of the forcefulness of this man, the pent-up power in him.

"Miss Eaton," he said in a quiet voice, "you have avoided a question."

"I was not aware of having done so, sir," Alicia said, getting to her feet. "I have made my point well enough, I think. You seem to have heard of Lord Taavis. You know the sort of unscrupulous man he is. You cannot believe that Randolph would be any match for him. Why, only this morning my cousin was telling me of some absurd plans that he has made to make use of Lord Taavis. As though he could! They threatened him last night, and he was frightened. But today he seems to have forgotten everything they told him. But I have not, sir. And I do not think you can be so heartless as to continue to allow Randolph to put himself in danger simply for the purpose of maintaining contact with the son of the local magistrate, who can, no doubt, give you all the legal scandal that you like."

"You really think that was why I made application to your cousin," Captain Hillary said, his dark eyes narrowed.

"I can think of no other reason," Alicia told him.

The captain raised his head and stared at the ceiling for a moment in silence. In the other room the sound of the presses seemed to become louder than they had been before. Alicia found that she was very aware of everything about her, the beam of morning sunlight which stole in the window, the summer warmth of the room, and the smell of books and paper.

"The question you did not answer," the captain said finally, "is whether or not Randolph took you with him to this meeting. That *would* have been a foolish thing, indeed."

Alicia knew she must be honest. "Actually," she said, "my cousin and I followed him."

She thought for just a moment that she saw the beginning of a smile. But then he was quite solemn again.

"I should have guessed," she heard him mutter. And then: "And may I ask, Miss Eaton, why you and Miss Fairbreaks did that?"

"I should think the answer would be obvious, sir," Alicia told him. "We were worried about his safety. Even his sister will admit that his judgment is not his strongest characteristic."

"And did you follow him straight into this deserted house?" he asked her.

"Actually," Alicia said, wishing that he would not press her to be so exact, "actually, we were invited in through a window at the back. We were standing on a shed roof, you understand . . ."

"Of course," he told her dryly. "Nothing could be more reasonable than that two young ladies should be standing on the roof of a shed behind a deserted house. This was at night, I take it."

"Actually," Alicia said, "it was."

"And of course it was only to be expected that you should be invited to join the discussion by one of the most notorious scoundrels in England."

"The gentleman is very charming!" Alicia said, losing her temper at last. How dare this man laugh at her! How dare he mock! "Yes, Captain Hillary, he *was* charming, which is more than I can say for you. And if you do not stop making use of Randolph, if you do not convince him to stop pursuing criminals at once, I will take the entire story to . . ."

"To your uncle, Miss Eaton? He constitutes what must be called the authority in this town, I think. I expect he will be very pleased to hear that his son is helping to uncover crime in Bath. Because surely that is your uncle's primary intent, as well. There are those who claim that all he does is try not to stir the waters. Or if he stirs them, only at the surface."

Alicia marched past him, her mobcapped head held high. "You are so interested in reform and principles, sir, that you do not think of the human element, sir," she told him. "You lack humanity, if you care for my opinion! Furthermore, now that I think on it, I would prefer to talk to a scoundrel any day."

CHAPTER TEN

On the day set for Lady Fairbreaks's entertainment, Alicia made her toilette with a sense of foreboding. Both Captain Hillary and Lord Taavis had, to her aunt's great pleasure and Alicia's complete astonishment, accepted their invitations, and after a great deal of harassment by Lady Fairbreaks, even Sir Humphrey had agreed to put in an appearance. All of which, Alicia thought, made for an explosive situation. She could only be glad that the affair was to be held in the afternoon, and as she donned her circassienne gown of green silk with its short puffed sleeves over longer ones and its stylish front fastenings of hooks and eyes, she told herself that no harm could come of a few people taking tea together of an afternoon.

Actually, to speak of a few people was an understatement. Lady Fairbreaks, working in close conjunction with her great friend Mrs. Tanner, had not been able to resist the temptation to make it clear that she had a wide acquaintanceship in Bath.

"Of course, Dorine," Alicia heard her say a score of times, "*you* would not have my problems, since you know so many fewer people. That is to say, you do not know many people well. If it were not that everyone knows we go about together, you would not receive half as many invitations. Which is all to your advantage, you see. Pray do not sulk when I am trying to cheer you! *You* would not have my problems with the guest list. *You* would not be faced with the difficulty of knowing who to include and who to keep out."

Mrs. Tanner appeared to be the perfect foil for Lady Fairbreaks's inflated ego. A pale, withered-looking woman who gave the impression of being ready to cast herself down in an instant and let anyone who wished to walk over her, she followed Lady Fairbreaks around like a faint shadow and was always ready to drudge in the most dismal way imaginable, whether it was writing her friend's invitations for her or supervising the cook.

Granted that Imogene had been of little use to her mother, for the very thought of once again seeing Lord Tommy, as she insisted on calling him, had thrown her into such a perfect tizzy that Alicia did not know what to make of her. Instead of being rude to her parents, Imogene contented herself with drooping about the house in a dreamy fashion at one moment and throwing herself into a whirl of activity—most of which concerned the dressmaker and her new gown—the next. On the one occasion when Alicia had tried to remind her that the gentleman she was obsessed with was of a questionable character and that, as the daughter of a magistrate, she would be risking a scandal if she were to show her favor, Imogene had refused to listen. Indeed, she had blocked her ears with her fingers, and Alicia had determined that she would not make another effort.

As for Randolph, she did not know what had happened. Had Captain Hillary summoned him and announced that he had no more need of his services? Alicia did not think that that was true, if for no other reason than that Randolph seemed to be in good spirits. Then, too, one day she had seen him talking to some of the people who had been brought up from the roundhouse by the watchmen, most of them members of the lower class who had either partaken too lavishly of liquor on the night before or, in the case of the ladies wearing red shoes, had attempted to make a living in a way which the law did not condone. She hoped that had been a sign that he had been dissuaded from trying to get information about Bath's underworld from Lord Taavis, but was discouraged by the hint it gave that he was still intent on investigation.

Whatever was going on, the only thing Sir Humphrey seemed to know about it was that there were repeated editorials in *The Gazette* to the effect that justice was a badly managed business in the city. From something that he said one day, Alicia took it that Captain Hillary had approached him by letter but that her uncle had determined to have nothing to do with the press.

"Damme, don't expect me to speak to the fellow!" he had told his wife only this morning. "I expect the only reason he is coming is to have a word with me. But I will see to it that he doesn't, I'll be a gudgeon if I don't!"

As for Lady Fairbreaks, she was full of her own notions. Lord Taavis should be aimed straight in Imogene's direction on every occasion. It seemed that she needed to know no more about him than that he had a title and appealed to her daughter. For the first time, Alicia realized how eager Lady Fairbreaks was to marry off Imogene and marry her well. She was glad that her own parents had never even hinted that wealth and a title should be the yardstick on which she should measure husbands. But her aunt made no secret of the way she felt. Indeed, she declared that she needed to know no more about the gentleman than she did. Sir Humphrey might grumble about his being a scoundrel but, as it turned out that he did not know much more about him, Lady Fairbreaks paid even less attention to him than usual.

Precisely on the hour, Alicia, with Imogene beside her, came down the stairs to help Lady Fairbreaks greet her guests. At her aunt's insistence, both girls had powdered their hair, and Alicia had even allowed the abigail whom she and her cousin shared, to pull her curls into an elaborate pattern. Imogene, in blue, looked quite attractive, and Alicia had hardly recognized herself when she had glanced at the pier glass. The circassienne gown, for which she could thank her aunt's generosity, was more fashionable than anything else she had ever worn and that, together with the new style of her hair, made her look pleasantly older than her years. Indeed, she realized she must be looking very well when, at the sight of her, her aunt had gone off into a perfect tirade in defense of her own beauty, which, she declared, even in maturity could not be surpassed.

The green salon was the largest room in the house, and it was here that the company was gathered. Little groups formed and reformed, making a swirling pattern when seen from the stairs. As though some magnet had control of her eyes, the first person Alicia really saw, even though he was at the far side of the room, was Captain Hillary. He was in close conversation with her aunt and Mrs. Tanner, but he chose that moment to look up, and their eyes met. It was, Alicia told herself as she and Imogene continued to descend the stairs, the first and last time she would look at him for the entire afternoon!

Lord Taavis was waiting for them at the bottom of the stairs, splendidly outfitted in a coat of cherry-colored velvet with a deep collar, his fair hair covered by a white wig made of the finest silk. It took only the single sight of him to send Imogene into such a quiver that Alicia was forced to press her arm quite tight in an effort to remind her that it was necessary to exercise control.

"And—and where is Mr. Bradshaw, sir?" Imogene asked him after the formal greeting had been exchanged. "I had thought to find him with you. I am certain that Mama sent him an invitation."

Again Alicia saw that thin smile which she had so quickly grown to hate. "It was my fault for not explaining the night we met, Miss Fairbreaks," he said in a murmur, "but the fact is that, although I allow for a certain informality in such matters as forms of address and things of that nature, Mr. Bradshaw is by way of being my servant. Granted that his duties are often unusual, but servant he is, all the same. I would not have been being fair to your mother if I had allowed him to come here as her guest, despite the invitation. You will explain this to her, I know."

Imogene colored, but it was clear that Lord Taavis was determined to spare her embarrassment. "As a matter of fact," he continued, "Mr. Bradshaw is probably better suited to be a part of this company than many of the so called members of the *haut ton* in Bath. Or London, for that matter. I do not wonder that you thought he was a gentleman."

Clearly Imogene was delighted that he had taken so much care of her feelings, and she was beaming as she introduced him to a few people here and there. Then Lady Fairbreaks descended on him, having reluctantly left Captain Hillary in the care of Mrs. Tanner, and welcomed him so profusely that even that debonair gentleman looked a bit confused. Imogene was sent off to fetch her father, who was standing on the other side of the room watching the proceedings with all the signs of profound disgust. And when it became clear that a daughter's pleadings could not sway him to agree to an introduction, Lady Fairbreaks went to make her own sort of persuasion, urging Lord Taavis to stay right where he was and allow "dear Alicia" to entertain him.

"This is precisely what I had hoped would happen," Lord Taavis said when at last they had been left alone. "I gambled on the chance that there would be some opportunity for me to speak to you in private here today. Indeed, it was the only reason I agreed to come."

Alicia was unpleasantly aware that Captain Hillary was watching her. Or perhaps it was only an accident that his dark eyes seemed to be resting on her thoughtfully every time she glanced in his direction. He had been joined by several gentlemen now, all of them addressing him eagerly while Mrs. Tanner slunk about in the corner behind. But Alicia could see that the captain's attention was no more absolutely on the conversation at hand than was her own.

"You are very adept at compliments, sir," she said to Lord Taavis in an absent sort of way. "How excellently you made my cousin feel that she and my aunt had not been gauche in inviting Mr. Bradshaw. I admired the way you did it."

All of which was true enough. For whatever reason, he had been kind. But she had no interest in him, other than . . . It came to her quite suddenly that here was an opportunity for her to find out whether or not Randolph had ceased to place himself in danger.

"Randolph is a remarkable fellow," Lord Taavis said, as though he had guessed her thoughts. "Look at him there across the room, talking to young Soupcon. You would not think he had anything more serious on his mind than the next ball or the pattern of the waistcoat he intends to order."

"And has he?" Alicia asked. "I mean to say, has he anything more on his mind? I thought you made it quite clear the other evening . . ."

"Have I said that you are looking quite sophisticated this afternoon, Miss Eaton?" he interrupted her. "Although why you need bother with powder and fripperies, I cannot but wonder, since you are, in truth, one of the most beautiful young ladies I have ever seen."

Something in Alicia tightened. Was this gentleman, like Captain Hillary, going to cut her off from all serious discussion? Was it true, as it was beginning to appear, that in society there was no room for a woman to be taken up in an intelligent conversation, no way for her to make her point unless, like Lady Fairbreaks, she developed an elaborate routine for tormenting her spouse? At home with her father and her mother, Alicia had never guessed at such a thing, for her mother's comments on all matters, even those dealing with the church, were considered by her father as earnestly as though they had been presented to him by another man.

"You will excuse me for having interrupted you to say that," Lord Taavis continued, with a narrow smile which had nothing to do with insincerity but which still troubled Alicia. "It only came to me that someone might come along and make it impossible for me to ever say it. Now as for Randolph, the reason that I said what I did was because he came to me the day after our encounter in that deserted house . . ."

He broke off, laughing. "You must have wondered why we chose to meet there," Lord Taavis told her. "The truth is, Mr. Bradshaw is a bit of a romantic. He seemed to think that such a gloomy setting would contribute to putting your brother off us. But it seems he was mistaken."

"You mean . . ."

"I mean, Miss Eaton, that Randolph came to me with the most extraordinary suggestion. I was to give him details about underworld activities in Bath in return for his seeing to it that my name and my activities were kept out of *The Gazette*."

Alicia looked at him, appalled. "I did not think he would do it!" she exclaimed. "What have you and Mr. Bradshaw decided to do about it?"

"That was what I wanted to ask you, Miss Eaton. What do you think would be the most effective response?"

Alicia wondered why, since this was the way she wanted to be treated, she did not have a better response.

"Well, if you do not have anything to hide," she told him, "I suppose you could simply disregard him."

His blue eyes were intent on her and he was still smiling. "But if we mean to introduce a faro table or any of the other sorts of gaming that Parliament declared illegal . . ."

"In that case," Alicia replied, "I do not think *my* advice is needed. I know nothing about illegal gambling."

"Except that your cousin could be in danger."

"But you have already implied that he is not. I mean to say, you do not seem to take him seriously."

Lord Taavis laughed. "I assure you, Miss Eaton, that I take seriously anyone who might make my move to Bath awkward. I take your cousin seriously, and Captain Hillary, too."

"I do not think we are talking to any profit, sir," Alicia told him. "At first I thought you meant to turn your mind to my concerns, but now I see . . ."

At which point she was interrupted by Lady Fairbreaks, who came dragging Sir Humphrey quite literally behind her. "My husband is so eager to meet you, Lord Taavis," she announced in the ripe sort of way women like her assume when they tell a social lie. One would have thought that Sir Humphrey had been willing to swim rivers and climb mountains for the honor, a possibility which his expression categorically denied.

"My honor, sir," Sir Taavis said in his smooth way, bowing.

Sir Humphrey could not bring himself to go as far as to say that, but he did extend his hand. At the same moment, Alicia saw Captain Hillary detach himself from the group of gentlemen with whom he was surrounded and come toward their little party in a determined way.

CHAPTER ELEVEN

It was an awkward situation, but Lady Fairbreaks seemed blissfully unaware of anything out of the ordinary. She only knew that she had managed to make her husband allow himself to be introduced to a gentleman of rank who might, with luck, become her daughter's intended. And if they were to be joined by the gentleman who wielded so much power of the pen by virtue of his control of *The Gazette*, why all the better. Later on she meant to try once more to convince Captain Hillary to expand rather than reduce the social column, and she was sure she would have her way. For the present it was enough that Lord Taavis should see that she counted the most important people in Bath among her friends.

And so introductions were continued. Sir Humphrey scowled and bowed to Captain Hillary and would, Alicia guessed, have made a quick departure if Imogene and Lady Fairbreaks had not managed to stand in such a special way that in order to leave the circle he would have had to push them both aside.

"You gentlemen have so much in common," Lady Fairbreaks gushed.

"If by that, madam, you mean that your husband imposes law, Captain Hillary means to reform it, and I to break it whenever possible, you are quite right, madam," Lord Taavis said lightly.

Lady Fairbreaks indicated by her laughter that she considered him to be a great wit indeed. "Oh, you will keep us on our toes, Lord Taavis!" she cried. "I can see that already."

Sir Humphrey expressed his view that that might be true in more ways than one, but before his remark could be addressed directly, Captain Hillary asked Lord Taavis if he intended to stay long in the city.

"As long as it is profitable for me to do so," Lord Taavis told him. "You know, perhaps, that gambling is my greatest preoccupation."

"Oh, not the greatest one, sir. Indeed, I hope not," Lady Fairbreaks said with a sly look at her daughter, who was smiling in a silly sort of way which was meant to indicate, Alicia guessed, that Imogene was love-struck.

"Well, of course, one does not count the ladies," Lord Taavis said graciously. "They are always highest on the list." His smile included not only Imogene but Alicia, although she refused to meet his eyes.

"I have heard it said," Captain Hillary declared, "that it is not out of the question that faro will be played at your private parties. They are to be called parties, I believe."

Lord Taavis showed as much amusement as was possible in pantomime. What a contrast in appearance he and Captain Hillary were, Alicia thought—the one so fair and dressed to the utmost degree of elegance in velvet, with his hair powdered; the other dark-skinned, dark-haired, and just as handsome in his coat of superfine, buff pants, and Hessian boots. It was informal wear for the occasion, perhaps, she thought inconsequentially, but no doubt he had come here directly from the newspaper office. Involuntarily she remembered being together with him in that small, sunny room so full of the scent of print and paper, and the dark hairs on his forearms which the pushed back shirt sleeves had revealed. It was an odd thing to remember quite so vividly, and she pushed the thought away with all the strength of willpower she possessed and made herself attend to the conversation.

"I am surprised to hear you mention faro," Lord Taavis was saying to the captain. "You have been abroad, I understand. The war must have proved a great distraction. No doubt you have forgotten, sir, that faro has been illegal for some time now, as well as deep basset, hazard, and ace of hearts. All games played with numbers used in a certain way seem to remain a constant displeasure to Parliament, although I have never understood the reason why."

"My dear Lord Taavis, I could not agree with you more!" Lady Fairbreaks cried.

"Madam!" her husband growled. "I hope I am

not about to have the pleasure of standing here and listening to you defend practices which are illegal. You strain my patience, madam. Indeed you do!"

"Why, sir, if you were to agree with her," Lord Taavis said dryly, "you would only have something in common with poor old Beau Nash. He died a broken man, I understand, and all on account of the result of the acts of Parliament on gambling in Bath. He is still a much admired man here, I understand, sir. And you, as a native of this city . . ."

"I am a magistrate first and foremost, sir!" Sir Humphrey roared, while all about them heads whirled and turned. "I am dedicated to upholding the laws of this country, sir, before all else! Beau Nash means nothing to me, sir. He died a pauper, I hear, and no doubt it was well deserved."

It was unfortunate, Alicia thought, that her uncle had been forced to take a public stand against a man who was so closely associated with the establishment of Bath as a spa that his memory was celebrated by most of the town's inhabitants. After all, it was he who, as master of ceremonies of the Assembly Rooms, had made Bath a fashionable center by insisting on making duels disreputable, improving many of the streets and buildings, and ordering the planting of handsome gardens everywhere, with the result that the *haut ton* had begun to flock down from London in droves, bringing Bath the prosperity that a spa with such a plentiful supply of spring water deserved, not to mention the Roman baths which had soon been discovered.

Granted, of course, that gambling had been Beau Nash's downfall, Alicia reflected. He had been a gamester from the start of his career, and when Parliament had outlawed the favorite games of numbers, over thirty years ago, he had, cleverly some thought, initiated gambling which used letters instead, particularly one favorite called Even Odd. Five years later, unfortunately for the gentleman who had once been driven through the streets of his city in a coach which was always drawn by six gray horses and announced by the blare of French horns, Parliament struck again, and this time he was ruined.

And now Sir Humphrey had spoken out against him. But then, of course, how could he do otherwise, when everyone knew that serious gaming was against the law? Alicia wondered how many of the company had heard about Lord Tommy Taavis, the gentleman scoundrel down from London to make his packet at Bath. Was her uncle aware of the threat the gentleman beside him posed, she wondered? Had he made special arrangements to have Lord Taavis's parties watched? The only thing she was certain of was that Randolph was working against his father, whether he realized it or not. No good would come out of all this, she realized with a shiver.

Her aunt still busily defending Beau Nash and gamblers in general, Alicia let herself think of the possibilities. Randolph could discover that Lord Taavis was promoting illegal gambling, in which case her cousin's life would not be worth a shilling. Captain Hillary could get the information that he wanted about the underground crime existing in Bath. Perhaps he might even bring charges against Lord Taavis. Was this, she wondered, why he was eager to meet the gentleman? And if he exposed him, or any other criminals, for that matter, how would it make her uncle look? Oh, it was all a tangle, and it was clear that at the moment her aunt was not making matters any better.

"I do not believe that you have answered my question directly, sir," Captain Hillary persisted. "Or can I take what you have said to mean that you intend to behave with the same freedom here in Bath that you have done in London?"

Lord Taavis shrugged. "Ah, well, sir, you know London no doubt as well as I. It is possible to do a good many things there if one knows the proper people."

With a sudden stab of insight, Alicia saw just what Lord Taavis intended to do. It was neither her beauty nor any particular attraction that he had for Imogene which had brought him here today. Rather—and she was sure of it—he had used Lady Fairbreaks's invitation as a way to compromise her husband at some future date! She was not certain yet just how he meant to do it, but she had never been more certain of anything in her life. Sir Humphrey was not aware of what was going on, although he scowled and grumbled. As for the captain, either he was unscrupulous enough to have solicited these public comments regarding Lord Taavis's practice of bribing people or else he was more heedless than she had thought.

Whatever the answer, Alicia knew that she must do something. A statement about bribery had been made. Her uncle was saying nothing. Imogene and her mother smiled blissfully upon the scene. And Captain Hillary was about to take the conversation further down some path or other. Alicia decided that she simply could not risk it.

"I am certain that Lord Taavis has never made a practice of bribing people," she said sweetly. "Or have you, sir? So many of the other guests are listening to this conversation that I think we must let them know."

She had chosen to be direct, and it gave her the advantage. Clearly everyone was taken by surprise. Granted that Captain Hillary only gave her one startled glance and that Lord Taavis took a step backward before he smiled, but she knew that she had set the occasion on its ears.

"Just in case all this has been said for the purpose of embarrassing my uncle," Alicia went on, speaking clearly, "I would like to remind all the other guests—and I think most of them are listening—that Sir Humphrey has never met this gentleman before. Indeed, he has only allowed himself to be introduced to him under duress.

And now who can blame him if he is offended by the fact that this gentleman—a guest in his own house—is boasting indirectly of how simple it is to get one's way in London illegally? As though he meant to do the same thing here in Bath. Which, as you all know, would mean that he hopes to bribe my uncle."

"What's this?" Sir Humphrey sputtered. "Bribe me, indeed!"

Alicia's mind worked quickly as she spoke. She saw a warning in Captain Hillary's eyes, but ignored it. Randolph, who had been lolling against the mantlepiece, had started forward and was staring at her with eyes which seemed to bulge a little. As for her aunt and Imogene, their smiles were fading as though their faces were painted with oil which, exposed to heat, begins to drip.

"The captain here would like nothing more than to learn that you could be taken advantage of," Alicia said as sweetly as she could. "It would make an excellent headline, I think. And Lord Taavis has made it clear that bribery is one of his many fortes. I suggest that later, after weeks have passed, there may be rumors that the parties at Lord Taavis's were not watched closely enough and that . . ."

"But you are joking, surely!" Lady Fairbreaks screamed. "The dear is just down from the country," she explained to the company at large. "And *such* an imagination, if you please! She makes a drama of everything! Now, no more serious talk! As your hostess, I command it. Sir Humphrey . . ."

"No one has ever accused me of bribe taking!" her husband cried, red faced and panting and clearly much confused. "What's this? What's this, I ask you?"

"My dear, let me help you to your study," Lady Fairbreaks said in a flurry. "You shall take a little rest and be quite calm again. Yes, yes, Imogene! You assist your father instead. After all, I am the hostess . . . Mrs. Tanner, do come here and talk to Lord Taavis. Don't tell me you are going, sir!"

"I am afraid I must, madam," Lord Taavis said with a gracious smile, bowing deeply to his hostess, for all the world as though she were not in a state bordering hysteria. How many other ladies had he left in this same condition for even better reason, Alicia wondered. It took no great wit or experience to guess that Lord Taavis was the sort to fade away when difficulties began.

Imogene gave a little cry of protest but could do nothing more to keep him, since her father was apparently verging on an apoplectic state.

"We will see one another again," Lord Taavis said reassuringly, including Alicia in the embrace of his glance as he backed with some considerable skill toward the door. "I will be sending out invitations directly for a little soirée of my own. Do not let the conversation we have just concluded distress you, ladies. Captain Hillary misses the war, no doubt, and would conjure up other battles on this turf. But he will have to look elsewhere for his editorials, I fear. Good day, Lady

Fairbreaks. It has been delightful. Miss Eaton. Ah, yes, good day, Miss Eaton! That part of it is a pity, surely."

And, without explaining precisely what his last remark had meant, Lord Taavis took his departure as a footman held the door, taking his tricorne hat from the servant as he went.

The party had been disrupted. A silence followed the closing of the outer door, and then everyone started to talk as close to simultaneously as was possible. Imogene and her father had disappeared in the direction of the study, Lady Fairbreaks was flying about from group to group making the proper noises associated with festivity, and Mrs. Tanner, woebegone as usual but making the effort as directed, was attempting to start a conversation with Captain Hillary.

However, although he replied to the faded little woman politely enough, Alicia could see that Mrs. Tanner did not have his attention and was relieved when someone asked her a question in passing, allowing him to turn away.

"Miss Eaton," he addressed her, "I must leave soon, as well, but before I do I think I should warn you that although Lord Taavis seems to be all charm and good manners, he is dangerous with women."

"With women!" Alicia cried impatiently. "Why, the gentleman is dangerous with everyone, I warrant! That was why I came to see you the other day. For Randolph's sake, he must have nothing to do with the fellow."

130

The thought of her cousin sent Alicia searching for him with her eyes. But he was gone from his place beside the mantel, and she could not see him elsewhere in the room.

"I have not forgotten a word that you have said to me, Miss Eaton," Captain Hillary replied. "And I hope you will keep my words in mind as well. Lord Taavis is no one to play games with. Under certain conditions, events could turn extremely ugly if what I anticipate occurs."

"If it does, sir, and if Randolph comes to grief," Alicia assured him, turning her green eyes on the captain in a penetrating way, "I will know where to lay the blame. I can assure you of little else but that."

CHAPTER TWELVE

It was evening before Sir Humphrey allowed himself to be mollified. Lady Fairbreaks, declaring herself exhausted, not only by the party but by the necessity of convincing her husband that no one suspected him of taking bribes, went up to bed, leaving Imogene to bend Alicia's ear concerning the many virtues of Lord Tommy Taavis.

Clearly love had provided her cousin with all the stimulation that she needed, and her spirits were high, but Alicia found herself in the grip of a depression which she could not raise. Granted that she had done what she could to prevent Lord Taavis from using her uncle, but everything else offered nothing but discouragement. Clearly Captain Hillary placed the newspaper first, and she still had no way of knowing whether or not he had so much as given Randolph any warning. Added to this was the fact that Lord Taavis seemed quite confident that he could do anything he liked in this provincial city, which was certain to cause trouble in the end. And it was exasperating that Imogene had chosen to idolize such a person. In the face of her cousin's glowing comments, what could Alicia say which would cause her to see the gentleman as what he really was?

"As far as playing faro and the like are concerned," Imogene went on blithely, "I think that altogether too much ado is made about it. I do not often agree with Mama, but in this case I do. What can it possibly matter what games of chance men and women play? One can gamble just as dangerously on whist, I fancy, if you place enough money on every point."

Alicia closed her eyes to indicate her lack of patience. Even straight up from the country as she was, she knew that games like faro and deep basset encouraged gentlemen to lose great fortunes. All one had to do was read the papers to know of the tragedies which could take place when a man did not gamble directly with a friend, someone whose character he knew, but placed his bets instead against the house.

Furthermore, it was common knowledge that organized gambling of the sort of which Imogene spoke attracted the worst elements of any society —pimps and prostitutes and petty criminals, desperate men and women willing to do anything for another chance at life. And in the face of all the evidence, here was Imogene, blushing and laughing and telling her that any sort of gambling was quite all right.

It was left to Alicia to propose that, as the daughter of the town's chief magistrate, it might

133

be better if Imogene were to keep her opinions concerning gambling to herself.

"Furthermore," Alicia went on, warming to her subject, "I do not think you should place too many hopes on Lord Taavis."

"You only say that because you think he is fond of you," Imogene retorted, stung. "But that is only because he is the sort of gentleman who always notices pretty ladies. He will find me sympathetic in so many ways, once he comes to know me, that he is bound to be intrigued."

Alicia could think of nothing to say to blunt her cousin's optimism. Indeed, since Imogene was soon going on about always knowing that she would live one day on the Royal Crescent, the conversation—if that is what it could be called— grew rapidly so fanciful that reasonable comments were out of the question.

"I was not going to mention it," Imogene said finally, having exhausted the subject of Lord Taavis's place of residence, "but it was too bad of you to suggest that he might want to make use of my father, Alicia. The idea would not have come into anyone's head if you had not proposed it. I can quite understand why Lord Taavis made such an abrupt exit. You are too suspicious, I declare!"

Alicia, knowing she could prove nothing, shrugged her slim shoulders. No one, it seemed, was prepared to understand her. And perhaps in the end she would be proved quite wrong. After all, what did she know of society, let alone gamblers down from London? No doubt that was the reason that Captain Hillary did not appear to take her seriously.

Although it was not that late, she was just preparing to go up to her bedchamber, as much to escape Imogene as anything, when a knock was heard on the front door and shortly a little maid scurried in to say that Mr. Soupcon was asking after Mr. Fairbreaks.

"Why, I imagined that they were together," Imogene declared, starting up from her chair in a whirl of muslin. "Ask Mr. Soupcon to come in, Agnes, do. Mind Papa is not disturbed. He is asleep by the fire in the other room."

The idea came to Alicia as soon as young Soupcon made his insouciant way into the room and lowered himself into a chair, slouching himself in such a way that only the high heels of his foppish shoes kept him in place. If anyone should know what her cousin Randolph had been up to, it was this young gentleman. But she must approach the subject indirectly, get him to give information without warning.

Instead, it was Soupcon himself who provided the subject for discussion. "You ought to worry about your brother," he told Imogene, assuming a less laconic manner than was usual by virtue of squinting up his eyes. "He's got himself into bad company. 'Pon my soul, I don't like to think of it."

"If you are referring to Lord Taavis, sir," Imogene said stiffly, "I cannot imagine any company I would rather see him with."

"It's worse than that. I'll be a peacock if it isn't," was young Soupcon's enigmatic remark. "Grant you that when it all started I was willing to go along. I'm a true friend to your brother, Miss Fairbreaks. You'll admit that isn't any lie. And if he wanted to play at working for a newspaper, I was primed and ripe to go along with him. But this is a different matter."

Far from having to coax young Soupcon to give up his secrets, Alicia realized it might be impossible to dam up the flood of information which was presently flowing from his lips. She could only be glad that her aunt had retired and that Sir Humphrey was safely snoring in the other room.

As for Imogene, it was clear that she was half impatient to hear what he had to say and fearful, on the other hand, that he would somehow oblige her to change her frame of reference, particularly in regard to Lord Tommy Taavis.

"If you and Randolph have secrets, sir," she told young Soupcon, "then you must keep them."

The young gentleman shoved himself up in his chair until he was nearly sitting upright. "I don't want it on my conscience if anything happens to him," he declared in such a forthright way that Imogene turned quite pale.

"Now you are going to be tiresome like Alicia," she replied. "Randolph could not be in danger in this town, sir. In the first place, everyone knows who his father is, and in the second . . ."

She was forced to pause for just a moment.

"In the second," she said finally, "this is not London. This is a civilized English spa. There may be footpads in the country and pickpockets here in town. But we are speaking of petty crime, sir, and there is no danger for him there, even if he does try to expose it. Or give it to Captain Hillary to expose."

Clearly she was trying to persuade herself. Clearly the only reply she wanted was a reassurance that she was right. It was equally apparent that young Soupcon could not provide for her in this tidy fashion.

"Struth, that is what I would have thought a month ago," he told her. "And a month ago it would have been quite true. But now that the word is out that Lord Taavis intends to open a faro table . . ."

"Why, there is nothing in that!" Imogene cried. "It is against the law, and well he knows it. It is only that he likes to joke about the subject. If he intends to have gaming at his house in the Royal Crescent, you can be assured that it will be of the legal kind."

Young Soupcon rolled his eyes, presumably in protest against such innocence. "If you are right, Miss Fairbreaks," he replied, "then the Rimrod Ring have been severely misinformed."

"The Rimrod Ring!" Alicia and Imogene cried together, and indeed, it had an ominous sound. The vague anxiety which Alicia had felt ever since her cousin had decided to involve himself with spying in the underworld was now resolved into a hard knot of terror.

"Real felons, all of them," young Soupcon continued, making no effort to reassure them. "I have it on good authority that when they heard about Lord Tommy Taavis and his plans for Bath, they took the first express and are right now establishing themselves somewhere in the city."

"But who are they?" Imogene exclaimed. "What do they do? Why have they come here? Is Randolph really in any danger? Where is he tonight? Oh, dear, I think I must wake Papa and tell him . . ."

Alicia put out a hand to calm her, even though she was feeling considerable distress herself. "Let Lord Soupcon tell us what he knows first," she said in as even a voice as she could manage. "It may be that there is no need for concern."

"Concern, Miss Eaton," the young gentleman lanquishing in the chair opposite declared. "Indeed, I believe there is every reason for alarm."

"Alarm!" Imogene cried in a shrill voice. "Did you really say alarm? This is no joke you and Randolph have schemed up together, is it? It would be like him to throw me into a perfect fit and then come in the door laughing."

"If he comes in the door at all tonight, I, for one, will be relieved," the young viscount assured her. "The Rimrod Ring is a group of felons, as I said, Miss Fairbreaks. All of them have been in prison at one time or another. They like to brag about it!"

"Oh, dear! Oh, dear!" Imogene cried in a fit of shivers.

Alicia rose and went to put her hands on her cousin's shoulders in hopes of calming her.

"Perhaps you should not be so explicit, sir," she said to the young viscount who, she suspected, was half enjoying himself. She was reminded, somehow, of a young boy in her father's parish who delighted in making his sister scream by holding up spiders and such during church service.

Young Soupcon threw himself out of his chair and let the mantelpiece support him. He was a lanky fellow and, despite his stylish dress, seemed never to know what to do with such troublesome appendages as his arms and legs, all four of which were very long.

"Well, of course," he said in a huffy way, "if you are not interested in my story . . ."

"I am vitally interested, sir!" Imogene assured him. "But, I declare, you do frighten me."

"Perhaps once we know more about the matter, there will be less to fear," Alicia observed, sitting down beside her cousin on the settee and smoothing her skirts as carefully as though she were quite calm. "Are you quite certain that you want to hear the details, Imogene?"

"Indeed I do," her cousin assured her. "You say that they are felons, sir. Convicted prisoners who have served their terms."

"And some, they say, who have not," the young

man told her, managing to looked extraordinarily doleful.

"And what do they mean to accomplish here at Bath," Alicia demanded. "They call themselves a ring, you say. How many of them are there?"

"Oh, any number!" young Soupcon told her, spreading his arms as though to indicate a multitude.

"Scores or hundreds?" Alicia said dryly, beginning to suspect that Randolph's friend was pretending to more knowledge than he had at his fingertips. Still and all, she wanted to hear what he had to say, since it appeared to be the only way they would learn anything about Randolph's secret ventures.

"Scores," young Soupcon said, clearly abashed. "I only said it was a ring, Miss Eaton, and not a mob."

"And who is their leader?" Alicia asked him, deciding that questions presented in an orderly manner would yield better results.

"Why, it is someone named Rimrod, I assume," the young viscount told her, clearly taken off guard.

Alicia rose and went across the room toward him. He was so tall in his gangling way that she had to tip back her curly head to talk to him.

"How much do you really know?" she asked him. "Come, this is not a time for games!"

"I know what Randolph has told me," he replied defiantly. "And since he was not very coherent when he reviewed the matter . . ."

"By that you mean that he was in his cups?"

"If you want to put it bluntly, yes," he told her. "It was last night, as a matter of fact, and we may have both had too much of some excellent bottles of claret. My father laid them down in '43."

Alicia had always suspected that young Soupcon found it difficult to keep his mind on any subject for long.

"And so it may be possible that you do not even clearly remember what you heard," she suggested.

"Clearly enough to tell you there'll be trouble," he told her. "These fellows have come down from London to create a bit of mischief. They have no respect for the law. And the fact that Lord Taavis has decided to make Bath his base has assured them that there is no strong arm to promote law and order."

"They have misinterpreted his coming here completely!" Imogene cried. "Of course Lord Taavis will respect the law."

Seeing that her cousin was in no mood to be reasonable, Alicia did not enter into an argument. "I suppose," she said, "you do not know what this gang is going to do."

"No more does Randolph," young Soupcon told her. "But he intends to uncover their entire operation. How he laughed about it when he told me. You see, he is certain that they will want a few loyal members here in Bath. People who know the ins and outs of the city."

"My brother intends to become a member of a

141

criminal ring?" Imogene demanded in a voice so loud that Alicia was convinced that Sir Humphrey would awaken.

"That is what he told me," young Soupçon said in the self-satisfied manner of someone who has made his point with all the dramatic effect he could have hoped for. "He intends to hint that he can get them special favor with his father."

"Oh, what a great fool," Alicia murmured.

"He says that he will do anything necessary to make them feel quite safe," the viscount told her. "Then, when they are well established and their defenses are quite down, he intends to go to Captain Hillary with the story. All he could talk about last night was the size of the headlines."

"If he does not have a care, his name will be featured in a headline, I fear," Alicia told them. "We must put our heads together and think of what we can do."

CHAPTER THIRTEEN

Although no doubt young Soupcon had caught the essential flavor of the Rimrod Ring, he had gone awry on some of the details. It was not true, for example, that they were all convicted felons. In matter of fact, only Frank Rimrod himself had ever been in prison, and that had only been because his single attempt at being a footpad in London failed, leaving him sprawled out in a street with an old gentleman beating him over the head with a cane and demanding his purse of money back.

Frank Rimrod did not like to remember his brief stay in jail. Certainly he had not found his sort of company there. Brought up a cockney within the sound of Bow bells, he was a rough-and-ready sort of fellow, but ambitious and ready to work for what he got. Behind bars, he felt himself one of the many failures England so casually produced in the narrow streets of her slums. Then and there he had dedicated himself to being different. If he were to be a criminal—and that was really the only way a fellow with his background could make a fortune—he would be a criminal with class.

Once released from prison, Frank Rimrod set about rounding up some fellows with like ambitions, and finally found them in the figures of Tom Whitley and Jack Farmer, two gentlemen who looked much rougher than they truly were. All of which was part of the reason that Frank chose them, for it was necessary, he thought, to impress certain people that it might be dangerous not to be agreeable. The second reason for Tom and Jack's selection was that, although capable of taking orders, they were scarcely competent to have any ideas of their own, although Tom, in particular, often tried. Despite Lord Soupcon's estimate of scores of followers, therefore, it happened that Frank Rimrod's ring was a ring of three.

Once the ring had been assembled, it had been necessary to consider what criminal activity they should be up to. Tom had been keen on what he referred to as "snatch and grabbing," but Frank Rimrod assured him that their subsequent activities would bear a different hallmark than those that had gone on before, when each of them had been independent.

So when he had heard that Lord Tommy Taavis was determined to open a faro table and introduce other forms of illegal gambling in Bath, Frank Rimrod thought he saw his opportunity.

"In the first place," he told his companions, "it has to mean the magistrate there can be bought."

The only difference of any consequence between Tom Whitley and Jack Farmer was that one of them was tall and the other was very short. Both were burly and pugnacious looking, the sort of men who are inclined to walk about with their shoulders hunched and their eyes peering in every direction, as though they expected to find enemies around every corner.

"You mean we is to go about buying magistrates?" Tom asked his leader now. "Why, I ain't never found meself in need of one before."

"There's a deal of things we will need when we is men of consequence," Jack Farmer told him, delivering a friendly thump on the shoulder which would have struck down a lesser man.

Frank Rimrod made no effort to explain that magistrates were not packaged and delivered on order. He was accustomed to being misunderstood and knew full well that if he were to pause at every opportunity to give vocabulary lessons nothing would be accomplished.

"Second," he continued, "serious gambling brings serious gamblers, if you understand what I mean."

Jack Farmer and Tom Whitley nodded their heads in unison and then looked at their leader in just such a way as to indicate that they were waiting for an explanation.

"I mean by that," he had told them patiently, "that there'll be services that they'll be wanting. Young ladies to keep them company of an evening after they've left the faro table, for example."

He accompanied this with a wink so broad that in any other company it would have been ludicrous. As for his companions, they caught the point and fell to a great slapping of their knees.

"There's some will need to borrow money with no questions asked," Frank Rimrod told them, glad to see them warming so quickly to the idea. It was necessary, he thought, to raise the question of where that money would come from, and he knew that they would not. They depended on him to think of everything, and indeed, Frank was sure he would.

So it had been decided to go to Bath directly, and Frank saw to it that rumor got about that the Rimrod Ring was about to descend on the West Country and could be positively contacted at a certain address as close as he could manage to Lord Taavis's residence at the Royal Crescent.

The trouble was that all the Rimrod Ring could afford was lodgings. Added to that was the fact that Mrs. Simpson, their landlady, was the interfering sort, whose philosophy was based on the misconception that by virtue of moving into her house, her lodgers had given her permission to intervene in their lives as well.

"I want you to know that I keep one of the most respectable houses in Bath," was her constant refrain. She was a narrow woman whose face looked as though a door had suddenly been shut upon it, and she spent endless hours pretending to dust the hall in order to be close to doors in the event that voices were raised sufficiently for her to overhear.

As a consequence, Frank Rimrod spent a good deal of time when he was in the house in reminding his two companions to speak in whispers. And since the memory of neither was what might be called outstanding, he seemed constantly to have his finger to his lips.

But hopes rose higher now that they were actually in Bath. After the prison and then London, the spa had a holiday air about it, and Frank was forced to remind himself more than once that he was here on business of a very serious nature, namely the promotion of crime.

But first it was necessary to find crime to promote. Frank Rimrod's first efforts to introduce himself to Lord Tommy Taavis met with dismal failure. Indeed, after his meeting with Mr. Bradshaw, Frank began to think that he had trusted too much to the bellicose appearance of Jack Farmer and Tom Whitley. Indeed, Mr. Bradshaw did not appear to be struck by them at all, even though, as they had been instructed, they thrust their chins out in a determined way and stretched their faces into horrible scowls.

Frank Rimrod recognized true meanness when he saw it. After all, he had not been in jail without learning something about men's dispositions. And he saw that, underneath his smooth surface, Mr. Bradshaw was a raging tiger. He could imagine him doing anything that was necessary to protect his master, while both Jack and Tom were squeamish at the sight of blood, even if it was they who shed it.

Well, that was class, and something for him to aspire to. Lord Taavis could have the best because he could afford it. He had come into *his* money, for which Frank Rimrod bore him no rancor. Some were lucky early, others late. He intended to be one of the latter.

While the Rimrod Ring remained in this indeterminate state, Randolph Fairbreaks appeared upon the scene like the answer to a prayer.

Mrs. Simpson brought him up the stairs, and it was clear that her suspicions concerning Mr. Rimrod and his friends had been put to rest by the appearance of the magistrate's son himself.

"Are you quite certain you do not desire tea, gentlemen?" she said in her best manner as the members of the Rimrod Ring stood staring at Randolph with open curiosity and some suspicion. Was it possible that the magistrate had heard of them before they had even begun their operations? And, if he had, why had he sent his son as deputy?

There was, of course, only one conclusion, Frank Rimrod decided as Mrs. Simpson took a reluctant leave, no doubt to station herself as close to the door as possible. He must remember to warn Mr. Fairbreaks of the need to speak very quietly, particularly since, as was certain, he had come here ready to accept his father's bribe.

As for Randolph, he was clearly nervous. The first gang to descend from London in Lord Taavis's wake must be taken very seriously indeed, particularly since he intended to ingratiate himself with the purpose of becoming one of their company.

Consequently, he was taken quite off guard when the little red-haired bantam of a man who was Frank Rimrod himself asked him straight out how much he wanted. It was an awkward moment, since Randolph had not thought of the possibility of the leader of a gang passing out a salary. The splitting of ill-gotten gain, on the other hand, was another matter. That was what he had expected. But to be asked how much he wanted when he did not even know the going rates of a budding criminal . . .

When he mentioned five shillings, Frank Rimrod stared at him in such a puzzled manner that Randolph knew he had made some breach of etiquette.

"In all?" the gang leader asked him. "Is that what you want in all?"

That was it, then. Randolph sighed his relief. Here he was, not even having to state his purpose. Frank Rimrod had guessed it at once and come straight to the point, and now even the matter of salary was clear.

"Every week," Randolph told him, laughing, eager to let this ruffian from London know that he appreciated his wit. "Ha Ha! That's a good one, pretending to think that was all I wanted.

And, of course, if things go well, I may ask for an increase."

This fellow was nothing if not direct, Frank Rimrod thought with a sudden chill. Not only could his father be bought, then, but he was already thinking of raising the rate when they were settled in their business. Well, that was fair enough, Frank Rimrod told himself. If he could not make contact with Lord Taavis immediately, it would do him a world of good to have the local law enforcement officer in his pocket.

As he and Randolph shook hands over the agreed amount of five shillings weekly, an idea exploded in Frank Rimrod's mind. Here was a way to make his first big stake. As other criminals came drifting down from London, he could put them in touch with Sir Humphrey—who certainly seemed to be a most moderate gentleman if his bribe was any indication—by way of Randolph. *He* would arrange the meetings. *He* would keep a record of amounts to be paid.

Just to be certain that he did not tread on Randolph's toes, he asked him now if it would be convenient to be paid here in Mrs. Simpson's lodging house every Thursday.

"'Pon my soul," Randolph declared. "Indeed it would." And he reflected that Frank Rimrod was the most obliging fellow he had ever met. Here he had just walked into the room and was not only offered a salary immediately, but encountered with a choice of days on which he preferred to be paid. And when the leader of the gang continued with the information that he expected to come up with some other gentlemen who would like to pay him as well, Randolph thought that he had never been treated quite so handsomely before.

Of course now there was the question of precisely what they wanted him to do for his money. It was only with an effort that Randolph forced himself to recall that this was only a clever gambit on his part to know the ins and outs of criminal endeavor. Soon he would have to reveal everything to Captain Hillary. But not too soon, surely. It would be better to give himself time. In the meanwhile, there was Frank Rimrod and all these other as yet unknown people waiting in the wings to give him money.

How proud his father would be of him when all was known, Randolph told himself on this occasion. He could hear the startled exclamation as Sir Humphrey opened his paper to see it all laid out before him, how his son had ingratiated himself with criminals in this fair city, risked life and limb perhaps, so that the law could be enforced.

At this point his meditation was interrupted by Jack Farmer, who had been sent out for a bottle of gin. This same bottle being subsequently passed from hand to hand by way of celebration, Randolph soon found himself in no condition to inquire as to the terms of his employment and was startled much later in the evening to find himself weaving his way down the South Parade, with his companions vanished and the empty gin bottle clutched in his hand.

Sleep caught him in a fond embrace before he could reach his bedchamber, and it was young Soupcon who found his friend slumbering on the steps of his house. Indeed, Randolph continued to sleep the sleep of the righteous and the just as young Soupcon, together with Alicia and Imogene, escorted him upstairs. If in the morning he had a jumbled memory of what had passed, there was only the gin to blame.

CHAPTER FOURTEEN

The next afternoon Alicia was taken by surprise when the little maid came to tell her that Captain Hillary was at the door, wanting to see her.

"I didn't know whether to show him into the drawing room or not, miss," she added, "seeing as the mistress is away from home and all."

Alicia knew that, according to the terms of the strictest decorum, she should not have a private interview with the gentleman. Not only was her aunt off on a shopping expedition, but she had taken Imogene with her, and as for Randolph, he had somehow managed to recover sufficiently from the excesses of the evening before to allow him to sally out just after noontime. Earlier Imogene had made some effort to discover what he had to say for himself to explain his condition of the night before, but Randolph had been successful in remaining incommunicado by virtue of remaining in his bedchamber and refusing to respond when his sister had pounded on the door. It had not escaped Alicia's attention that he had waited until Imogene and his mother had left the house before hurrying out of it himself.

As for herself, she had pleaded a megrim in order to give herself time to think. What young Soupcon had told her and her cousin the night before about Randolph's involvement in criminal activities had seriously disturbed Alicia. Unlike Imogene, she did not suffer even the slightest delusion about Randolph being able to take care of himself. And if, as had been reported, he was closely involved with the activities of a gang down from London, a gang consisting of scores of hardened criminals, then there was no anticipating what might happen. Lord Tommy Taavis was bad enough, but all he had done was to threaten Randolph not to trouble him any further. The leader of the Rimrod Ring might not bother with a warning if he were to find out Randolph's real purpose for working with him.

All this she had been fretting over and over in her mind as she sat in the sunlight pouring through a window of the smallest parlor and pretended to be working on her embroidery. It was clear to Alicia that Randolph was in quite serious danger. And yet what could either she or Imogene do? To confide in Lady Fairbreaks would be worse than futile. It was clear that Randolph did not intend to discuss what he was doing and would probably be put out if he were to know what his friend Soupcon had told them. As for the possibility of going to Sir Humphrey, that, Alicia thought, might turn out to be a double-edged sword. On the one hand, he might be able to extricate his son from trouble by breaking up the ring, once he knew that it existed. But what if even one member of it eluded the grasp of justice? Randolph would be in dire danger, since it could only be assumed that he had been his father's informant.

It was a puzzle, then, to which Alicia had been able to find no answer. Granted, she had thought of Captain Hillary. But nothing had seemed to come of her last visit to his office. It had simply given him another chance to condescend. And certainly after the way she had attacked him at her aunt's soirée the other afternoon, he would not be in a mood to entertain other requests from her of the same nature.

And now he was waiting for a word with her. Alicia knew she must put Randolph's well-being before anything else, even decorum. Given the confidential nature of the news she meant to give him, she could not even request that the door be left ajar.

"I believe he must have come about the newspaper account he means to write about Lady Fairbreaks's entertainment," she improvised to the anxious-looking servant. "I know she is looking forward to seeing it in the earliest possible edition. Given that, I think I ought to see him. It is a small matter, strictly business, and I know that Aunt would want it."

The lie came out so smoothly that Alicia amazed herself. Was that to be another outcome of her stay at Bath then? Was this still another of the bad habits she would return with to the country? It was strange that whereas at her father's vicarage a lie would simply have meant endless complications, here in Bath it seemed to smooth the way.

She was just putting aside her embroidery hoop when Captain Hillary was shown into the room. "Thank you, Nelly," Alicia said as briskly as she was able. "Pray shut the door. Good afternoon, Captain Hillary. I am sorry to receive you alone, but my aunt and cousins are out. I assume that it must be something of importance to have torn you away from your busy schedule."

Alicia scarcely recognized the sound of her own voice. Certainly she had never meant to sound quite so sharp. Objectivity was what was wanted now, and how quickly she seemed to lose that quality whenever she was with this gentleman. First she must find out what he wanted, and then if it seemed the right thing to do, she might tell him something about Randolph's new difficulties. After all, if Captain Hillary could be useful, why should he not be used?

One glance at him told Alicia that he was looking at her strangely. His deep-set, dark eyes seemed to be exploring her face as though it were a strange territory which he could not quite define.

"I—I am sorry to have sounded brusque," Alicia said by way of apology. "Do sit down, Captain Hillary, and tell me the nature of your visit."

"You were right when you said that it was a matter of some import," he told her, not accepting her invitation, although she sank onto a chair. "At your aunt's entertainment the other afternoon you made it very clear that you thought I was taking advantage of an opportunity to put your uncle in the wrong."

Alicia bit her lip and said nothing. It was better to remain quite silent, she told herself, until she could discover in which direction he meant this conversation to go.

"Now, at the time the full significance of what you said did not strike me," he continued. "I mean to say, your outburst took me by surprise. I accounted it to the hostility which you apparently feel for me and have ever since our first meeting."

To her own amazement Alicia found that even while he was speaking about something which clearly concerned her greatly, her mind would wander off to that morning in the newspaper office just off York Street. Today it was clear that he had come straight from there, for there was a touch of printer's ink on the wrist ruffles of his lawn shirt. She remembered again, so clearly, how he had stood looking down at her, much as he was doing now, and how his shirt sleeves had been turned back and the neck of his shirt open. . . .

"I cannot account for that hostility completely," Captain Hillary was saying now. "But that is not the point. I have decided that I cannot let you or anyone else think that I cold-bloodedly tried to make it appear that your uncle and Lord Taavis had or were about to come to any arrangement. In fact, I have done what I can to prevent such talk, which must, of necessity, have been encouraged by the mere fact that Lord Taavis was invited here."

"That was my aunt's decision," Alicia murmured. "She—she does not understand the situation."

"Yes," he replied. "That is how I assessed the matter. Certainly it was clear that Sir Humphrey was not at ease. But, as I was saying, I made no mention of the guest list in *The Gazette,* as you may or may not have noticed, Miss Eaton."

"My aunt is certain that is because you mean to write a full-fledged article, describing the afternoon from firsthand observations," Alicia told him.

"There will be no article," he told her, "full-fledged or otherwise, and I will be happy to tell your aunt that myself. But we have strayed from the central subject, which is your mistaken belief that I want to stir up trouble."

Alicia tried to protest, but he did not give her the opportunity. The anger which he must have hidden at first greeting her was in evidence now in the glint of his dark eyes and in the turn of his head. There was, Alicia thought, no condescension now, at any rate.

"All along, Miss Eaton," he continued, "you have persisted in mistaking my intentions. I have

158

reason to think that there is a criminal element in Bath which has gone largely undetected. Whether this is the fault of your uncle is not the question. This town is growing. A good many people like Lord Taavis will soon be coming here, and some without such charming manners."

"I am quite aware of that, sir," Alicia told him, stung into speech by his implication that Lord Taavis's "charm" meant anything to her one way or the other. "In fact, I may know more than you do about it. Unless, that is, you have heard of the Rimrod Ring."

For once she had taken him off guard, Alicia saw. Indeed, he took no pains to pretend he was not startled.

"The Rimrod Ring," he repeated after her. "I have never heard of any gang with such a name. Tell me, Miss Eaton, where did you hear of them?"

How little it took to set him to condescending, Alicia thought. It was in the way he phrased the question, a turn of his voice. Or perhaps she was being too sensitive as far as Captain Hillary was concerned. Besides, the important thing was to somehow help Randolph, and if he could do so, then she was prepared to overlook a great deal. Or so she told herself.

"My cousin's dearest friend told my cousin and me that he was certain Randolph was mixed up with them," she said in a measured voice. "Randolph let it slip out when he was in his cups last night. They are a group just down from London, and there are a good many of them. Scores, Mr. Soupcon said."

"Strange," Captain Hillary said with narrowed eyes. "Strange that I should not have heard something of them. I have my sources now . . ."

"I'm sure you have, sir," Alicia said in a cool voice. "And if Randolph were not one of those sources you refer to so blithely, he would not be in his present danger."

"So we are back to that, are we, Miss Eaton?" Captain Hillary said wearily. "Bound and determined to blame me for everything your cousin does."

"*You* were the person who invited him to gather information for you," Alicia reminded him, leaping from her chair. "*You* were the person who took the liberty of listening to our conversation that morning at the Pump Room. As soon as you heard Randolph say what he did about injustice, you could not wait to talk to him. And your proposal caught his fancy. He is nothing but a romantic boy in many ways. Now because he fancies himself a secret agent or something of the kind, he is risking his life among strangers. All of them hardened criminals, I understand."

"I cannot think that we have had an invasion of felons in such a number, Miss Eaton," the captain said in a dry voice. "However, I take your point about your cousin. If I had guessed that he would play this drama out as though it were a farce, I would never have made his acquaintance in the first place."

"The least you can do is to tell him that you have no more need of his services," Alicia told him with her bell-clear voice. "But I asked you that the other day at your offices, if you remember. I all but pleaded, and as I recall, you promised nothing."

A cloud must have passed over the sun, for the room was suddenly in shadows. When the captain spoke, he was so detached that he might already have left the house.

"I did not know you wanted promises, Miss Eaton," he said in a low voice. "However, whether you care to believe me or not, I have had no word from Randolph, seen no sign that he believes himself to be working in my behalf. But certainly I will speak to him now and tell him that he has my advice to cease any association with the criminal element here at once."

"Are you certain, sir, that it will not be too much of a temptation to have him remain a member of the Rimrod Ring so that you can obtain information?" Alicia asked.

She had gone too far. She knew that as soon as she said the words. With an impatient gesture, Captain Hillary took up his tricorne from the table where he had set it and quickly left the room. Alicia did not know why she stood quite still and rigid until she heard the front door close behind him, but she did. And when all sounds had died away, she heard her own deep sigh.

CHAPTER FIFTEEN

It took Lady Fairbreaks's fancy the next morning to visit the shops which lined Pulteney Bridge. When Randolph did not come down to breakfast, neither she nor Sir Humphrey showed any surprise, and Alicia was reminded that the pattern of his ways was well established now. The family did not expect him to join them when they were making plans for the day, for it was frequently necessary for him to sleep off the excesses of the night before.

As for his relationship with the Rimrod Ring, the three young people had decided the night before, prior to Soupcon's finding Randolph asleep on the stairs, that they could do little more than urge him to confide in them.

"As long as we know precisely what he is doing, we can keep him from getting into danger," Alicia had declared, sounding more confident than she really felt.

"It will do no good to criticize him," Imogene had said. "The more we criticize and warn him, the less he will let us know."

"I can always get him in his cups again," young Soupcon had said with more relish than was necessary.

"It would be better not to have the information than to get it that way," Alicia had protested, and later, after struggling to get Randolph undressed and into bed, his friend had admitted to the two girls that he would not be acting as a friend if he encouraged Randolph in the direction of the bottle.

"Unless, of course," he had taken care to add, "it might save his life."

Alicia could only hope it would not come to that. Young Soupcon's limited information about the Rimrod Ring had made her feel so anxious in the extreme that she could only hope that Randolph would be sensible. The afternoon before, Captain Hillary had seemed to listen to her. But how could she be really sure that he had done anything to prevent her cousin from associating with criminal elements?

Nothing mattered to Captain Hillary except his newspaper, she told herself. All that he cared about was making his exposé. She had known from that first day at the Pump Room that he was single-minded. Everything that had happened since only substantiated her opinion. It would do no good to go to him with this new information. All he would say, no doubt, was that she should keep out of it. After all, the last words she had had from him was to warn her to stay away from Lord Taavis.

However, it was too bright a morning for Alicia to indulge in bitterness. As she and Imogene followed in Lady Fairbreaks's wake along Stall Street, which was crowded at this hour with carriages of all sorts and sedan chairs bringing people to take the waters, she could not help but feel that the night before had been a bad dream.

There was a pause in front of the abbey when Mrs. Tanner appeared, looking as doleful as usual in her gray pelisse and bonnet, to engage Lady Fairbreaks in a conversation. Obliged to watch the crowd, Alicia found her interest drawn by a red-haired fellow who strutted like a rooster and was followed by one very tall and one very short companion, both of whom hunched their heads forward and darted looks around them in the most peculiar way. She was about to draw Imogene's attention to them when her cousin clutched her arm.

"There he is!" Imogene exclaimed sotto voce. "Oh, dear! Do you think he will take notice? Or will he pass us by? Is my gown becoming? I would have taken more bother if I had thought for an instant that he might be passing by! Only watch the easy way he carries himself! One would think he had lived in Bath all his life."

It was true enough that Lord Tommy Taavis was striding along the crowded street with uncommon confidence, his coat thrown open and his thumbs stuck in the armholes of his waistcoat in such a way as to demonstrate a carefree manner. His handsome face was graced with a broad smile, which did not find a mirror in the countenance of his companion, the faithful Mr. Bradshaw, who was busy looking about in a watchful manner.

In an attempt to attract attention, Imogene was now rising up and down on her slippered toes, and when this tactic did not seem sufficient, threw herself into a fit of laughter so loud as to cause those closest about her to involuntarily raise their hands to their ears.

Alicia scarcely noticed these maneuvers, attracted as she was by another little drama which was being played out across the street. Her cousin Randolph, whom she thought they had left home abed, had appeared beside the red-haired gentleman who had reminded her of a rooster, and had embarked on an earnest discussion. The short and tall gentlemen, who appeared to be of a pugilistic nature, listened with scowls which might have indicated their determination to understand what was being said. Pretty soon the red-haired fellow began gesticulating, and then Randolph pointed at Lord Tommy Taavis, who had stopped to buy a nosegay from one of the girls who hawked them on the corners.

Imogene was still laughing so hysterically that Alicia was obliged to break off from her own considerations and shake her cousin by the arm. But the ruse had been successful after all. Lord Taavis's attention had been caught, and in a moment he and Mr. Bradshaw were at their side.

"La!" Imogene exclaimed, nearly exhausted by

her efforts. "My cousin is so amusing that some-times I cannot contain myself. What must you think to find me in such a fit of laughing, sir?"

Mr. Bradshaw might hold his own as some sort of equal in shabby rooms in deserted houses, but clearly, in this social setting he preferred to make a point of his position as an underling, for he stepped behind his master and assumed the ex-pressionless features of the sort a butler might have envied. Lord Taavis, on the contrary, became very expansive.

"I am indebted to Miss Eaton for being so wit-ty," he said with a deep bow. "Otherwise I might have somehow missed you ladies, and that would not have done at all."

Alicia thought it would have done very well, but she said nothing. Imogene was clearly in her element, and even though she was no beauty, she had glow enough to make her seem like one. If she noticed that Lord Taavis glanced at her com-panion more often than he did at her, she gave no sign. Instead she embarked on a long and com-plicated recitation of what she had been doing and what she planned to do, almost as though she were sketching an itinerary which would allow him to find her at any given moment of the day.

While her cousin was talking, Alicia looked back across the busy street, past wagons and car-riages and sedan chairs, not to mention pedestri-ans of every description, to where she had last seen her cousin with the odd threesome. The red-haired man and his odd-looking companions were still there in close conversation, but Randolph was gone. It was clear that their attention was focused on Lord Taavis, and that there was something vaguely ominous about it.

It was no more than could be expected, Alicia told herself. No doubt Lord Taavis had brought serious gambling to Bath. No doubt criminals of every sort would follow, although, frankly, she had expected people more dangerous in appearance than the rooster and his friends. And then remembering what Soupcon had told her and Imogene, it came to Alicia that the very fellows she had her eyes on might be members of the Rimrod Ring.

"You appear to be distracted, Miss Eaton," she heard Lord Taavis saying in his teasing way. "Or perhaps you do not find our company sufficiently of interest, which, I think, would be a pity, particularly as I was about to invite you and your cousin to a soirée at my house on the Royal Crescent."

Lady Fairbreaks had remained talking with her friend Mrs. Tanner close to the abbey, but although she was at a distance to put her quite out of earshot, a certain intuition seemed to alert her.

"Good heavens, I did not see you, Lord Taavis!" she declared, billowing down upon them with Mrs. Tanner cowering in her wake. "You must meet my dearest friend. But, I forget, you were introduced to her at my house the other day. Still, people are not likely to recollect introductions to her. Not, that is to say, the way they remember me."

"Yes, madam. You are quite unforgettable," Lord Taavis assured her with so much irony in his voice that Alicia flushed for her aunt, who fortunately did not appear to notice that she was being gently mocked.

"Lord Taavis was just mentioning an entertainment he is planning," Imogene told her mother in tones so sweet as to seem to drip sugar at the edges. Alicia reflected that she had never heard this particular tone in her cousin's voice before when she was addressing a member of her family.

"I mean to send a formal invitation, madam," Lord Taavis announced expansively. "You, your husband, your . . ."

"Ah, but you must not plan on Sir Humphrey," Lady Fairbreaks told him. "He is so busy defending this city from its criminal element that he rarely goes out of an evening."

In this case, Alicia told herself, her uncle was quite certain to refuse to appear in the house of a notorious gentleman scoundrel. It had been bad enough that he had been forced to have Lord Taavis in his house. It would be even worse when he discovered that his wife and daughter were going to promote the impression that there was a connection of considerable familiarity between his family and a well-known gambler who did not pay too much attention to which games were legal and which were not.

Lord Taavis did not seem quite so genial when

168

he heard that Sir Humphrey was not to be part of the Fairbreaks package. Alicia was not certain how he did it, but quite suddenly he was a little distanced, as though he had taken two steps backward, although, in truth, he had not moved. It was clear from Imogene's anxious attitude that she was conscious of it, too.

"Mama!" she cried, tugging at Lady Fairbreaks's arm. "Papa will do anything you decide on. Now you know that is true! You must promise me that he will agree to attend!"

"The dear child thinks there is nothing I cannot do!" Lady Fairbreaks declared, preening herself and arching her neck in a certain way she had when feeling very full of herself. "And it is true, of course, that my husband takes my advice in most things. Indeed, my friend Mrs. Tanner agrees that I am one of the most influential women in the city, don't you Dorine?"

Mrs. Tanner seemed to fold into herself like a fan to have the attention of the little group focused on her in this way. In a small voice, however, she agreed that Lady Fairbreaks was, indeed, formidable. Whereupon Lady Fairbreaks countered with the announcement that if her only daughter wanted her father in attendance at any particular occasion, then she should have him!

Lady Fairbreaks was so flushed with triumph, so voluble in the anticipation of her coming victory, that it was all Lord Taavis could do to get away. This he finally accomplished, not without having first taken the opportunity of suggesting to Alicia, in a very low voice indeed, that he was looking forward to seeing her again with the greatest anticipation. Alicia had bitten her tongue to keep from saying that, if it had not been for the debt she felt she owed her aunt, she would not consider setting one foot in his house.

On their subsequent progress to Pulteney Bridge, Lady Fairbreaks and Imogene kept up such a torrent of excited conversation and Mrs. Tanner attended to them so closely that Alicia was quite free to pursue her own thoughts. Certainly she did not think it wise that Imogene should be so impassioned by Lord Taavis. Clearly, even if he were not a scoundrel, he was not to be trusted in matters of the heart. Furthermore, she dreaded the scenes which were certain to take place if Lady Fairbreaks undertook to persuade Sir Humphrey to go to Lord Taavis's house. *The Gazette* was certain to seize upon the story and blow it up into something it was not. People were sure to begin to murmur stories about special arrangements being made to protect Lord Taavis's gaming interests.

So intent on her thoughts was Alicia that she had lingered behind on the porticoed walkway of the bridge while the others had gone into a draper's, which was only one of the many shops which blocked all view of the water. When someone spoke her name, Alicia started. Looking up, she saw Captain Hillary riding a handsome bay. No doubt he was returning from a gallop on the hills beyond the river and had thought he must

pause and greet her to be kind, to doff his tricor-
nered hat as he was doing now and . . .

"I am sorry that we parted on such angry terms
the other day," he said in a low voice. "I would
have wished, Miss Eaton, that you could have
greeted me with something other than a frown."

"I am sorry if my expression does not please
you, sir," Alicia retorted. "It is, I fear, the only
one I can muster at the moment."

How familiar the dark eyes and face seemed to
her. It was absurd, of course, for he and she were
nothing more than strangers. And what did it
matter how well he sat upon a horse, or how the
superfine of his blue jacket strained across his
powerful shoulders? And why was she reminded
of that moment in the sun-strewn office off York
Street with the presses pounding and his shirt
rolled to the elbow? It was nonsense, Alicia told
herself. Nothing but nonsense from first to last!
The only thing that really mattered was whether
or not this man had really listened to her when
she tried to tell him that there was a catastrophe
afoot for Sir Humphrey and his family. Particularly Randolph.

At least she could ask him. Had he talked to
Randolph or not? And if he had talked, had he
persuaded? Knowing Randolph, she knew that
this was the important part.

"Have you ordered Randolph to stop his interfering?" she demanded. "Has he separated himself from the Rimrod Ring?"

"I have talked to your cousin, Miss Eaton," the

captain told her as she bent her head back, letting her red curls scatter on her shoulders. "But he is playing some game or other. He would only say that he would have a great deal of information for me in the future, and when I told him that I did not wish to gather information at the expense of his safety, he gave me a wink and left my offices. I say this to you fairly. I can think of nothing further I can do."

"But what about this gang from London?" Alicia demanded. "What about the Rimrod Ring?"

Captain Hillary's dark eyes were hooded. "I confess that my contacts could tell me nothing of them," he said in a low voice.

"And so Randolph is still risking his life!" Alicia cried. "You have done nothing to prevent it! That is unfair, sir! You owe him some protection!"

With that, she whirled about and ran into the draper's shop, leaving Captain Hillary to stare after her thoughtfully. By the time she and her aunt and the others had come out of the shop ten minutes later, Alicia was relieved to find that he was gone. She expected that in appealing to him once again she had made another futile gesture. But at least when catastrophe came—and she was certain that it would—Captain Hillary would bear the full share of the responsibility.

CHAPTER SIXTEEN

"There is no use going on about it, madam," Sir Humphrey said in tones of grim determination. "I do not propose to attend. Further, not you or Imogene or my niece will accept that invitation. Give it to me and I will put it on the fire."

Giving a little scream, Lady Fairbreaks thrust the white folded paper so deep into the bosom of her gown that even her husband did not dare pursue it. "Really, my dear!" she exclaimed, "you do say the most outrageous things. Of course you will be going to Lord Taavis's party. So will all of us, I'm sure."

"I cannot be prevented from attending," Imogene declared, managing somehow to look like Joan of Arc making her preparations to be tied to the stake. "Why, it will be the most brilliant evening Bath has known in many months! Besides that, I have a special reason . . ."

"I do not want to hear about your reasons, you silly girl!" her father shouted, pounding the table with the gavel which for some reason he had brought in from his office when the last case of the day was tried. "Silence! I will have silence!"

"The only place you can legally demand silence is in your court, Papa," Randolph observed. "In your domestic household your rights are limited to a forceful request."

"Tempt me to be forceful, will you!" Sir Humphrey cried, making an effort to jump up from the table, the gavel still clenched in his hand. "You would be surprised to know how far a man can go in his own house, you young rascal! Only look at you! What do you think you are about, giving me advice! The only thing you are good for is to run up bills at the tailor's, bills which I am then expected to pay!"

"I have my own money now, Papa," Randolph told him. "You may not have noticed, but I pay my own bills now."

"That bodes no good," Sir Humphrey complained. "Make your own money, do you? Doing what, I ask? Sometimes I think I would prefer Bedlam to this household!"

Watching him rub his forehead, Alicia sympathized. The moment Lady Fairbreaks had suggested that he attend Lord Taavis's entertainment tonight, her uncle had made a lucid explanation of the reasons why he could not let any one of them accept. Now, from the top of his black horsehair wig to his square-toed shoes complete with copper buckles, he was the picture of an angry and dispirited man.

"I assure you that Bedlam will be quite the

174

better place, sir," Lady Fairbreaks told him, looming large from her place at the other end of the long table, "if you do not agree to accompany us tonight. Why, I put off the telling of it until now so that you would not be put to any bother. It was to be a spur of the moment thing, as far as you are concerned."

Sir Humphrey glowered at her from behind the uncut loin of lamb, Lady Fairbreaks having broached this subject just as they sat down to their three o'clock dinner. It was the family's custom to always reserve some battle or other for that time of day when they broke bread together, and it was still a phenomenon which made Alicia marvel, remembering as she did the quiet meals she and her parents had shared together and the remembered sound of laughter.

"Spur of the moment!" Sir Humphrey shouted. "That is the time allotted, madam, for me to throw away my reputation? I wonder that you give me that long, indeed I do!"

"All this business about reputation is just so much nonsense, Father," Imogene said with her usual parental regard. "Lord Taavis may like to be referred to as a gentleman scoundrel, but that does not mean he is a criminal."

"A criminal is one who breaks the law, gel."

"And just what law has he broken?"

"None, so far as your father knows!" Lady Fairbreaks said with an air of triumph. "Why, sir, just because he spoke jokingly of faro banks does not mean that he intends to have one. He only meant to rattle you a bit, and I cannot say I blame him, you are so dreadfully grim."

Sir Humphrey inclined his head. "I have a good deal to be grim about, madam," he muttered. "Miscreants during the day and a rebellious family to follow. The fact remains, not one of the members of this household will go to the Royal Crescent tonight."

Confusion followed, Randolph declaring that for "business" reasons he must be in attendance. As for Imogene, she kicked her heels against the chair legs and began to howl. Lady Fairbreaks rose from her chair with a dreadful slowness, nose, bosom, pointed finger all aimed in her husband's direction.

"I *will* go there, sir," she said in a voice which could just as well have been coming from heaven. "And so will your children and your niece, if they choose. Everyone of any importance in Bath will be there, and what excuse could I make to stay away? What would I tell Mrs. Tanner? That my husband had refused to let me go? Refused! Oh, I can imagine how quickly she would spread the word. She has always been jealous of me and my independence."

"You are not independent, madam," Sir Humphrey told her. "You are my wife."

"Piddle!" Lady Fairbreaks told him. "Piddle, twiddle, twaddle! I may be your wife, sir, but other than that, I am what I want to be!"

"I can take certain measures," he assured her, his face a ghastly purple as he leaned forward over the loin, his gavel still in hand, as though he meant to beat their roast to death, forgetting that it had already died.

"Lock the doors?" Lady Fairbreaks taunted him. "Shut the windows? Put the servants on guard? Or did you plan to beat me into submission, sir?"

The thought of her uncle, that little man in too large clothing, laying a finger on her formidable aunt was so absurd that Alicia might have been thrown into a fit of giggles if the circumstances had not been so fraught with dire consequences. Even Imogene and Randolph had been silenced at the sight of their parents locked in what appeared to be a mortal combat.

"If I go without you, sir—and I assure you, I mean to go—the entire city will know that I am there against your wishes. It is not the sort of occasion at which you could be absent without causing comment. It is all very well for you not to attend the Assembly Rooms or the concerts or an evening at Mrs. Tanner's. But if you do not appear at Lord Taavis's, you will have made a public comment."

Silence followed. Steely-eyed, they watched one another. Outside in the little garden there was the sound of birdsong, striking an ironic note. Alicia wished it would soon be over.

"I will make that comment, madam," Sir Humphrey told her, his eyes bulging in an alarming manner. "By my absence I will disapprove of Lord Taavis and everything he stands for."

Alicia saw a small smile touch Lady Fairbreaks's lips. It disappeared as soon as it had come, but she saw the cause of it immediately. Whether Sir Humphrey realized it yet or not, his wife had won a point. As matters stood now, she would attend the soirée and he would not. The first step had been taken, the first blow struck. Sir Humphrey did not realize it, but he would soon be tottering in his tracks.

"Very well, sir," Lady Fairbreaks said with her finger still pointed as though an invisible point extended from it which kept her husband hovering over the neglected loin. "Express your disapproval by not attending. I cannot prevent you from doing as you like. But you should be conscious that, as a consequence, you will become the butt of people's humor. They will laugh at you behind your back, sir. What sort of magistrate can you be, they will ask themselves, if he cannot control his wife? How are we to respect his dignity when his wife goes her merry way and consorts with people into whose houses her husband will not . . ."

Alicia did not listen to the rest of it, struck by the cleverness with which her aunt had turned the argument. Surely that was the case Sir Humphrey himself was making not too long ago. And now it was being used against him. She saw him falter, sink back in his chair. And then she knew that all was lost. Sir Humphrey's wits were frazzled. Something in his expression told her that he knew there must be something he could say, and yet he could not think what on earth it was.

"Once people begin to laugh," Lady Fairbreaks went on, pressing her advantage, "there will be no end to it, sir. You will not dare to go out on the street, and as for prosecuting criminals, what do you think will be the case when both they and the watchman are so convulsed that they cannot attend to the sentencing?"

"Damme, I will make them attend!" Sir Humphrey told her, but it was, at best, the last cry of someone who has been defeated. "I will pass such judgments . . ."

Now came the time for Lady Fairbreaks to heal the wounds. She was not an entirely heartless woman, and as long as she held the whip hand, she could be kind in her own rather brutal way. She informed Sir Humphrey, who was now slumped in his chair, that there were certain advantages to being seen at Lord Taavis's.

"People will take it that you intend to keep a close eye upon the gentleman," she said with a cheerful air. "They will remark to one another that you do not intend to close your eyes, as some magistrates have been known to do in London."

Alicia thought it equally likely that the citizens of Bath might think their chief magistrate was either signifying approval of illegal gambling or had been bribed, but this was no place for her to add a comment, even though it made her heartsick to see her aunt go unchallenged.

"After all, Papa," Imogene said, entering the

scene of the late fray on her mother's footsteps, "you have no proof that Lord Taavis intends to have a faro table. I think myself that he makes jokes about it but that is all. He likes to think of himself as something of a rogue, no doubt. It is the fashion. But in time you will see that he is someone you can admire."

Alicia wondered if it were possible that her cousin had forgotten that evening when they had overheard Lord Tommy Taavis threatening her brother. Could she have put behind her the atmosphere inside that dusty vacant room? Could she really have compromised in her mind the knowledge that Lord Taavis would soon be up to no good, even though it might not already have happened?

"As for keeping Lord Taavis in hand, Papa," Randolph announced with unusual energy, looking very self-important, "I think you can be assured that I can see to that quite nicely. The fact of the matter is that I have a certain influence in many quarters. Not that I intend to burden you with details."

"Spare me the details," Alicia heard Sir Humphrey groan. "And as for your damned influence . . ."

Again his voice broke, and he rose with all the heaviness of a much older man and left them.

"He will feel better in an hour," Lady Fairbreaks said in a good-natured way. It was clear from her flushed cheeks and bright eyes that winning battles acted as a tonic for her. "Randolph, will you carve the loin? We will save your father some of the most tender pieces, and after we have eaten, I will take it upstairs along with a glass of porter. That will raise his spirits."

Alicia found that she could remain silent no longer. "Aunt," she said, keeping her voice even with an effort, "do you really think it is wise for my uncle to be seen in Lord Taavis's company? I know that you and Imogene are taken with him, but . . ."

"My dear child!" Lady Fairbreaks cried as Randolph attacked the loin. "He is taken with us! That is the entire point! Nothing could be clearer than that, with the slightest encouragement, he will offer for your cousin."

"Well, as for that," Randolph grumbled, pausing with knife in hand, "I would count on nothing. Besides which, I intend to make such use of the fellow that by the time it came to marriage, he would have no reputation left."

What little appetite Alicia had ever had, had long since departed. No one seemed to notice when she rose and left the table.

"I cannot think what you might have to do with Lord Taavis's reputation," Lady Fairbreaks was saying as Alicia approached the door.

"Randolph likes to put on airs," Imogene said with a warning glance at her brother. "There is nothing more to it than that, Mama."

Alicia left them to reassure one another if they could. As for herself, she had decided that she wanted nothing better than to return to the country as soon as possible, to put all this behind her. If Captain Hillary thought he could attack corruption, she told herself, then he must start in every household, find the scheme behind every smile. She had come to Bath to be introduced to society, and now she felt somehow that she knew it all too well.

CHAPTER SEVENTEEN

Lord Taavis's house on the Royal Crescent was like all the others on the outside. Greek columns rose on either side of the door to form a porch of sorts, and the long windows did not differ from those of their neighbors. But once inside, there was a difference in the degree of luxury found in the thick and ornamental carpets, the lush velvet of the drapes, the paintings by old masters, all in their golden frames, and such beautifully crafted furnishings that each piece seemed a work of art. Add to this any number of Adam fireplaces of beautiful design and ornamental ceilings of every kind, and the sight was enough to make even Alicia catch her breath.

By this it must be understood that she had been determined not to be impressed. Indeed, she had badly wanted not to be in attendance and had intended to plead some small indisposition, until she realized that the balance of her aunt and uncle's relationship at this point was so tenuous as not to admit any added complication.

True to her word, Lady Fairbreaks had delivered Sir Humphrey at the proper hour. Suitably dressed in a pale blue satin coat and breeches which seemed to have been fitted to a much larger man, he had made a pitiful, defeated sight as he had stood on the doorstep to await the carriage which had subsequently taken them up the hill to the Royal Crescent.

In the light of the flambeau which was set outside the door, Lady Fairbreaks had appeared in her most magnificent apparel, all silk and satin with the usual deep décolletage made more impressive by the bones and lacing of her bodice and the full pleating of her skirt. Her powdered hair was raised a foot in front and at the back was turned over a pad before having been twisted into a knot on top of her head. Feathers were stuck everywhere until she resembled some exotic bird of paradise, and there was some doubt once she was inside the carriage that there would be room for anybody else.

Eventually, they were all packed in neatly, however, except for Randolph, who was forced to share the driver's seat. Once they had joined the other equipages of every variety on the Gay Street hill, an air of excitement managed to communicate itself so violently to Imogene that she fell into a shaking fit, which occasioned the application of a vinaigrette to her nose and her mother's demand that she take hold of herself.

As Randolph declared from his high perch, all the *haut ton* appeared to have been invited. "Nothing could beat this in London," had been his comment as he had handed his sister down and helped her disentangle the hoop of her lilac satin polonaise from the stone hitching post which chanced to be in the way.

"We should all take a lesson from Lord Taavis," was Randolph's comment to Alicia as he helped her down. "'Pon my soul, if this isn't the way to live, I don't know what is!"

Alicia had preceded her aunt, uncle, and cousins into the house, not on purpose, although she hated to see her uncle's face at the last moment, but because she was separated from them by the crowd. Lord Taavis, who was standing at the head of the curving stairs to welcome his guests, took advantage of the fact that she was unprotected by raising her gloved hand to his lips and protesting with more warmth than was necessary that now that she was here the evening could come to life. Alicia snatched her hand away but not before she had seen Captain Hillary standing in an alcove watching her, a strange expression which might have been one of mockery on his dark face.

"And so," she heard Lord Taavis say, "your uncle has been persuaded to come. I see him below on the stairs."

"You did not do him a kindness to invite him, sir," Alicia told him, aware that his hand was on her arm now and that he was holding back the other guests in order to make conversation with her.

"Come, Miss Eaton. You think too badly of

me," Lord Taavis began, but Alicia moved on as quickly as she could, only to find herself engulfed in such a mass of perfumed humanity, which thronged what appeared to be a very large salon, that she could only move with the utmost difficulty.

Suddenly a path was being cleared before her, however, and she found herself following in the wake of a gentleman in dove-gray satin, someone whose strong shoulders gave him away, even though his back was to her.

"Thank you, sir," Alicia said to Captain Hillary when they had reached the shelter of the alcove where she had caught sight of him before, an alcove which overlooked the stairs. "I see that you are well stationed to observe the identity of everyone who arrives. Tell me, will we see our names printed in the social column tomorrow or will they be emblazoned in a reforming editorial? And you might explain as well, as long as you are about it, why you saw fit to rescue me from the crowd."

"A simple thank-you would have sufficed," he told her dryly, his dark eyes making a rapid sketch of her face before he turned to observe the company ascending the long curve of the stairs. Among them Alicia saw her aunt and uncle, the one triumphant in her feathers and the other looking as though he wanted nothing better than to cut and run.

"I would thank you if I thought you were disinterested," Alicia told him, "but as matters stand,

I can only believe you made my way here for a purpose. Something which will suit you."

He did not answer her directly. "Lord Taavis seemed most solicitous when he gave you his greeting," he said in a low voice.

"I cannot be blamed for the gentleman's attitude," Alicia retorted.

"Most ladies like to think they can," he told her. And then, quite suddenly: "I admit to being surprised to find your uncle here, Miss Eaton. How does it happen? Can you tell me?"

It was an opportunity which Alicia did not know whether to take advantage of or not. If she were to tell him, quite honestly, that Sir Humphrey's attendance could be explained by the fact that he had fallen a loser in a domestic battle with his wife, would Captain Hillary believe her? And, even if he believed her, could she trust him not to make some sort of slurring reference in an editorial? Refusing to be put in a helpless position which might result from honesty, she chose to continue her attack.

"If you had chosen to play the part of gentleman, sir," she told him, "you might have talked this matter out with my uncle long ago. He could have told you his position. You could have told him yours. If you have some special knowledge concerning Lord Taavis's present activities, you could have let him know and have allowed him to prosecute, which, I assure you, is something he would not hesitate to do."

"You do not have a high opinion of me, Miss

Eaton," the captain murmured, "and indeed I am sorry for it. As a matter of fact, I thought you might be aware that all my applications to see your uncle have met with dismissals of such a sharp and sudden sort that I have the opinion that either he has a special distaste for newspaper editors or he has something to hide."

Alicia had not known of Captain Hillary's specific applications, and the knowledge might have softened her if it had not been for the fact that at this very moment her uncle was being required to exchange a bow with his host.

"Somehow this could have been avoided!" she heard herself exclaim.

"Your uncle does not look as though he is enjoying himself," she heard the captain murmur. "No doubt your aunt and cousin's happiness will make up for his apparent distress."

He had come too close to the truth for comfort, although Alicia could scarcely blame him. Certainly her aunt looked as though she had swallowed several canaries baked in a rich sauce, and Imogene quivered like a volcano about to go into eruption.

"And then, of course, your other cousin," the captain went on, scarcely moving his lips. "No doubt he is up to something, as usual, but I would be hard put tonight to know precisely what it is."

Indeed, Alicia herself had noticed a certain pent-up excitement in Randolph tonight. She had credited it to the fact that he might think this visit brought him close to the very heart of Bath's new underworld. Surely, however, if that were the case, he would have already been disenchanted. All the *haut ton* of Bath was in attendance. In a moment, if he had not already noticed, he would see Captain Hillary. That should be enough, surely, to convince him that there were no secrets to be dredged out tonight.

"But you said before that all this might have been avoided," the captain continued. "Was that only one of those remarks ladies throw out to tantalize, or will you tell me what it means?"

The fact that, under any circumstances, this gentleman could confuse her with ladies in the general sense, threw Alicia into a fine fury. Her face grew as pink as the color of her polonaise and then as white as the flounced petticoats beneath it as she turned on him in all her slender beauty. She made a quaint picture, although she did not know it, with the scoop of her décolletage rimmed in silver lace in contrast to the ivory of her neck and shoulders. The red flame of her curls drawn up on top of her head in a pretty fashion with a green bandeau was only faintly misted with powder.

"I am offering you no provocation of the sort you hint at," she told him. "I sincerely meant that it makes me sorry to see my uncle placed in this awkward situation. At least Lord Taavis could have made his purpose in coming to Bath more clear. Either he means to do as he has done in London—set up illegal gaming tables and resort to bribes to keep in operation—or he only means to keep within the law as far as gambling is concerned."

The captain's eyes were very dark. Dark eyes, dark face, dark smile against the silver contrast of his powdered hair and his cravat. "As long as the matter is uncertain, your uncle would have been well advised not to have seemed too friendly with the gentleman," he said.

"And well he knows it," Alicia said, fury producing honesty at last. "But he has his private worries which you know nothing of. Actually, my uncle has private worries which concern his wife and daughter. There, have I provided sufficient grist for your mill? You have used my uncle's son, sir, and now you can use me to add to the flood of gossip."

"I do not deal in gossip, Miss Eaton," he told her. "Much as it distresses the ladies of this city."

"I wish you would put a stop to all this talk of ladies!" Alicia told him, stamping one small satin-covered shoe. "Every time you say the word, it is all too clear that you think us an inferior product. *I* am not distressed by the fact that you claim not to deal in gossip. I care nothing for it myself."

"If you would hear me out, Miss Eaton."

"Hear you offer your excuses!"

"If you will. Call them anything you like. I am sorry if your uncle has been forced to come here as part of some domestic squabble. I am even more sorry to see you here yourself."

"That should not concern you," she said tartly.

"I am quite sure that you are right," he made

answer. "It should not, although it does. But as to the matter of your uncle, I simply said that he had been unwise. You have told me all I need to know about his reasons. . . ."

"I was right, then!" Alicia cried. "That was the only reason you rescued me from the crowd. You wanted information. First you used Randolph, and now you are using me!"

And before he could stop her, she had stormed off in a perfect passion, from which she did not recover until she encountered Randolph, who appeared to be looking about for her.

"Mama could not think where you had got to," he told her, "but I had seen you and Captain Hillary all cozy together and I said . . ."

"I hope you did not say *that* to her!" Alicia cried. "And, as for being cozy, we were anything but that. He thinks your father has made a grave mistake in coming here, considering that this house promises to be the scene of private parties which will feature illegal gaming. I tried to explain that it was a private matter, that what Lord Taavis would soon be about was quite beside the point, but . . ."

She was usually not so outspoken, but her interview with Captain Hillary had shaken her, and she would have gone on and on, no doubt, even though Randolph seemed distracted, if Mr. Bradshaw had not put in an appearance.

"Lord Tommy'd like the pleasure of talking to you in private, Miss Eaton," he said in a rough undertone. "Once the party's going on its own,

191

in a manner of speaking. Perhaps if I could just show you the particular room. . . ."

Although the fellow was clearly trying to show her every dignity, all Alicia could remember was that evening when Lord Taavis had helped them through the window. Mr. Bradshaw had looked dangerous to her then, and he did not appear to be much changed.

Still, Alicia told herself, there was no need to be frightened. Lord Taavis's romantic motives were more than clear. She was aware that he was a scoundrel. Surely he had told everyone that himself. And she could not afford to meet him alone, even if Imogene never knew. Still, she would like to talk to him in private. Ask him his intentions as to gaming. Assure him that he could not bargain with her uncle. Convince him, perhaps, to go back to London and let them rest in peace. Anything was worth the gamble. And yet she did not want to compromise herself.

"I will be glad to meet the gentleman if my cousin can be in attendance," Alicia said and waited for Randolph to state his agreement. Surely this was what he wanted. Whatever brought him closer to Lord Taavis and his doings was greatly to be desired.

But Randolph had been drawn to one of the low windows which lined the columned salons and was looking out of it with great attention.

"I do not think a tête-à-tête with you and your cousin was quite what Lord Tommy had in mind," Mr. Bradshaw admitted with an uncertain air.

"Come, sir. Surely he could not have thought to insult me by thinking that I would meet him unaccompanied by any chaperon," Alicia said quite clearly. "Randolph, I want you to come with me to another room where Lord Taavis wishes to speak to me presently."

Somewhere in the crowd, Alicia knew that her uncle was fuming while her aunt and Imogene waited for their host to finish greeting his guests and come to find them. Instead Lord Taavis wished to speak to her, and she was not at all certain what he could have to say, particularly if she was accompanied. Would that alone spoil his plan? Meanwhile, however, she could take advantage of the situation. No matter what his response might be, she would feel that she had done *something* to prevent catastrophe. And with Randolph there . . .

"Randolph!" she said again, more sharply. When he still did not turn away from the window, she murmured an apology to Mr. Bradshaw and went to stand beside her cousin. "Randolph," she repeated, "I need a favor of you. What on earth do you find so distracting?"

He tried to edge her away, but it was far too late for that. The salon they were standing in was on the second story of the building, running from front to back. The window that they were looking from therefore commanded a view of a back garden which ended in a slope. Twilight was descending, but it was far from dark, and Alicia was able to distinguish three figures below her approaching the back of the house. There was something familiar about the little group, although she could not think what on earth it was. One man was tall, the other short. The third had a cocky stride. Then her attention was claimed by Mr. Bradshaw, who suggested that she and her cousin follow him, and Alicia turned her attention to more important matters than that of shadows in a garden.

CHAPTER EIGHTEEN

Frank Rimrod had thought of the possibility of making an event of Lord Taavis's entertainment, but all that Tom or Jack could think of was some sort of grand snatch and grab.

"If it was winter, that would be a possibility," Frank told them, trying to keep the impatience out of his voice. "I mean to say, the ladies would have a room to leave their wraps in and we might pick up a bit of fur and perhaps a reticule or two. But being as it's summer, there's no good in it unless you want to go on the market with some scraps of cashmere and a bit of lace."

Still, he knew they needed to take advantage of something soon. It was all very well to pay that fellow Fairbreaks weekly for the privilege to operate in his father's legal domain without fearing an arrest. But what good was immunity to them if they did not commit any crimes? Frank had not even been able to make his point to Lord Tommy Taavis, although he had certainly tried. The closest he had gotten to him was that fellow Bradshaw, who had indicated in no uncertain terms that they did not need anyone's protection, least of all when the contact was Randolph Fairbreaks.

Now, of course, Frank understood why. He had seen Sir Humphrey getting out of a carriage, which meant that Taavis already had him in his pocket. Well, that was none of his business really. As long as he had his own access to the judge, what did he care about any other arrangements that had been made?

Back at their hideout, as Tom and Jack liked to call the rooming house, he had come to a decision earlier, the decision which they were about to carry out. Frank Rimrod only wished it had not been so difficult to make his point clear to his two companions.

In the first place they had had to waste a good deal of time making certain that Mrs. Simpson was not within listening distance. They had first become aware that their landlady had a penchant for eavesdropping when she had suggested one afternoon, when setting out their dinner, that she would feel it an honor if Mr. Rimrod could familiarize her with some of the "London language" which he sometimes used.

"For instance, there's the word 'millken,' " she had asked him in a speculative way one morning when she had come up with the breakfast tray. "What does it mean, I wonder?"

Only slightly suspicious, Frank Rimrod had told her that it was a familiar way of referring to a housebreaker among the criminal class. But when she went on to ask him about 'buttock-and-file,' which she seemed pleased to learn meant a shoplifter, and 'bridle-cull,' which passed for a name for highwayman among the underground, Frank realized that these were not words she was apt to come across in the ordinary way. Indeed, it was coincidental that these very terms, among others, had been used the evening before when he and Tom and Jack had had a talk about old times over a tin of ale from the nearest corner shop.

However, if it was true that she had listened to them reminisce, Mrs. Simpson did not seem particularly shocked. More garrulous than usual, she had confided to Frank Rimrod that she preferred gentlemen as boarders.

"Not as particular as the ladies, men ain't," she had declared, continuing to linger at the door. "And if they're quiet and respectable appearing, I wouldn't ask no questions in the ordinary way."

Whether or not she was issuing a general invitation to have her home become the permanent quarters of the Rimrod Ring, Frank did not know. But he set about at once making inquiries, only to discover that the now defunct Mr. Simpson had been suspected of being a bit of a smuggler when he and Mrs. Simpson had lived in Bristol. At least that was the story. The facts were that, his health having failed him, he had let his wife bring him here to Bath and set up lodgings.

"Must seem a bit tame here after Bristol," Frank had hazarded shortly after, only to find

Mrs. Simpson ready to be more than frank about her husband's doings.

"It don't matter who knows it after all these years," she told him, having issued the invitation that he join her in her sitting room for a glass or two of porter which she had on hand. "Can't convict a man for nothing when he's gone and pegged out like Albert's done," she told him. "Fact is, it brought in a pretty penny without much work attached, not as you'd want to mention. There's no knowing how well off we might have been—Albert and me—if he'd been bright enough to organize a ring."

She had let the suggestion dangle temptingly, making Frank more certain than ever that she knew about the Rimrod Ring and was, quite indirectly, giving it her full approval.

"I could have helped him in a good many ways," she had gone on wistfully, which for some reason had made Frank shiver and claim that he could not take another glass of porter, not if his life depended on it.

The odd thing about it was that Frank should have felt more at home in the rooming house, making his plans and knowing that Mrs. Simpson, if she knew of them, was certain to approve. But the fact was that it made him edgy to think that maybe just outside the door stood someone determined to be his nemesis. Indeed, he was convinced that if their landlady had so much as a hint of their plans, she would insist on being part of them, just as she had been part of her husband's operation in the Bristol Channel.

And so the Rimrod Ring whispered. At least when they remembered. When Frank first made the suggestions, Tom Whitley had sworn a great oath which had echoed against the walls, and Frank had been forced to clout him about the head and shoulders to keep him from saying even more aloud. And when he had gone into the details of it, Jack Farmer had protested in such a determined voice that Frank had been down on his hands and knees before him, begging for silence.

The fact that it was kidnapping set Tom and Jack a little sideways.

"Snatch and grab is one thing," Tom Whitley mumbled. "I'd stake my life on snatch and grab. Why, I was brought up on it. My old dad . . ."

When Tom got off on his old dad, there was no stopping him, so Frank waited impatiently, and Jack Farmer, who had heard it all before and was not one to put on a show, fell fast asleep. Later, the story over, they had to shake him by the shoulders, and once his eyes opened, the first thing he could say was that he meant to have no part of it on moral grounds.

This, of course, was too much for Frank to take. He did not know that Jack had ever stood upon a moral ground in all his life. Indeed, it would come as a surprise to him, he said, to discover that Jack knew what the word meant. The fact of the matter was—and he put this very forcibly—

that they could not call themselves a ring and enjoy such privileges as paying for protection if they were never to commit a crime. As for snatch and grab, he added, he wanted to hear no more of it. If snatch and grab had been all they had been after, they could have stayed in London.

Tom and Jack, however, were still in a rebellious mood. Their consensus seemed to be that when you dealt in human traffic, someone was likely to be hurt. Now there was nothing wrong with punching, in their books, and Tom had once twisted a man's nose until it had turned black and blue. But there were certain limits. A kidnap victim was a living witness—someone who could identify and bring charges. As a consequence, it stood to reason that they should be eliminated, once the ransom was paid.

"Damme, if it ain't the safest way," Jack Farmer said, taking his gin with a good appetite. "It's no good returning them after the money's changed hands. Before you have a chance to spend it, the law is down on you. I've heard of it happening time and time again."

"That's what makes the eliminating necessary," Tom Whitley said to Frank with the air of one teaching a lesson to someone simpler than himself. "And eliminating's always a bloody business."

At that Jack Farmer announced that there were exceptions. "You can put them in a bag and drown them," he announced as Frank resisted the temptation to bang his head on the wall.

"Now, I've done that with kittens. Mind you, I never liked it, but I done it. First you want to fetch some stones, and then . . ."

Frank was conciliatory, because it was clearly necessary. His ring might fall asunder at any moment, leaving him with Mrs. Simpson and a lodging bill which she had been gracious enough not to present, as yet, but which, at the first hint of his leaving, she was certain to have drawn up in a hurry. He suggested that the sort of kidnapping he had in mind was little more than a simple game. Someone would be restrained, but with the greatest kindness. A ransom would be requested, not demanded.

"If you ever hear me say the word 'demand,' you can quit the venture," he told them. "What we mean to do is give the Rimrod Ring a hallmark, in a manner of speaking. Let the world know how we do a job, so that when people begin to come to us with commissions . . ."

At the word "commissions" Jack's moral outrage began to fade, and Tom Whitley granted that there *were* limited possibilities to snatch and grab. "It might as well be a person as a purse, I'll grant you," he mumbled. "And there's more gold in a ransom than any purse would hold, I reckon."

Frank Rimrod was relieved to see the rapidity with which they came about. It was his own true conviction that a reputation was everything. Only look at Lord Tommy Taavis. There was no need for him to take lodgings with a smuggler's widow.

No, indeed! He could command a fine residence on the Royal Crescent, and someone like Brad Bradshaw to lend a bit of class to his endeavors. Now, granted, he had a title and, no doubt, an inheritance as well. It was usually that way with the aristocracy. It was, indeed, what made them different.

All this he explained in detail to his two companions. "But with us it's a matter of having to start from scratch," he told them. "And that means a big crime is best. Now, I don't fancy murder."

Great groans from Tom and Jack Farmer indicated that the thought appalled them as well. Tom declared that it was a bloody business, and Jack Farmer declared that he could not stand the sight of gore. It only took a butcher's shop to make him as light-headed as a lady without her vinaigrette.

Frank reminded him rather sternly that he was *not* a lady and, further, that since they were not to follow that particular course, there was no use in discussing it. Their identity would be kept secret by masks throughout, he told him. The person kidnapped would be handled with the greatest care, but never once see their faces.

"Then when the ransom's paid, the person can be returned at once, no more the wiser than anyone else who was responsible," he concluded.

Tom and Jack Farmer mulled it over, weighing the pros and cons to the best of their limited capability.

"Who you got in mind?" Jack demanded in the middle of their consultations. "Can we pick at random? Tom says that then it will be more like snatch and grab and . . ."

"If we pick at random," Frank said with a sour expression, "who will we send the ransom note to, eh? I fancy you didn't think of that. Which, I might add, is the reason why you need a leader."

His companions considered him with the respect Frank felt he deserved, and the gin bottle was passed again to everyone's satisfaction.

"The problem is," Tom Whitley noted, "we haven't made acquaintances. Damme, if we don't know who anyone is, we're in a pretty tangle."

Frank said dryly that he scarcely thought they could begin to associate with the *haut ton* without drawing some attention. "But you're wrong about our lack of acquaintance," he told them. "There's the man we pay five shillings to a week. And there's his son."

Jack Farmer indicated that if Randolph were his son and someone took him, he would not be all that eager to get him back.

"I'm thinking of the sister," Frank interrupted. "Imogene's her name. All we need to do is get her schedule from her brother. Pick her off like a cherry from a tree. And we all know what she looks like. Mind that day before the abbey? She and her cousin were talking to Lord Tommy, and I took the pains to point her out."

Tom Whitley indicated that, given his druthers, he would rather take the cousin. "Don't do no harm to have the victim be good to look at, does it gov'nor?"

But Frank Rimrod had refused to consider abducting Alicia. "According to Randolph, her father's a poor country parson," he told them. "And her uncle may or may not want to pay a price to get her back. No, there's nothing better than to strike Sir Humphrey where it hurts."

At that point Tom Whitley had succumbed to confusion. "It don't seem right, somehow," he told them. "We've paid our five shillings, and we rates protection. But we can't expect Sir Humphrey to honor that part of the bargain if we've got his own daughter in custody. Or can we?"

Frank had explained that it was at this point that Randolph could come in handy. "He can assure his father that his sister is in good hands," he told them. "Let the old gentleman know she's safe and all of that. No need to say how he came by the information. No doubt Sir Humphrey would trust his son with his own life, let alone his sister's. When we're ready, we'll send him our demands, written down all proper. I'll do it myself with my left hand."

"That's the ticket," Tom Whitley said, giving Jack a nudge. "The boy will come in handy in more ways than one."

"And when the money's in our hands," Frank told them, "the young lady is returned. Why, I declare, I don't know why I didn't think of it before."

"Let's hear it for our leader!" Jack Farmer cried.

"Let's hear it for the Rimrod Ring!" Tom Whitley shouted.

Outside the door, Mrs. Simpson, whose hearing was very good indeed, hurried off down the narrow stairs to the echo of a chorus of hip-hip hurray!

CHAPTER NINETEEN

"Surely your cousin can remain outside, Miss Eaton," Lord Tommy Taavis suggested in a mellow voice, standing very tall and handsome in the elegant library to which Mr. Bradshaw had led Alicia and Randolph. "After all, I sought only a brief interview. I must get back to my guests."

"Randolph remains," Alicia said, taking one of the wing chairs beside the desk in a flounce of white muslin and ivory satin. Tonight she had drawn her red curls close to her head with a green silk bandeau and the effect was charming. One look at Lord Taavis told her that her looks might not be to her advantage. Clearly he was a man who made advances to young ladies when and where he saw fit and was not accustomed to refusal. All the same, she intended to turn the tables on him. *He* had had her brought here for a brief assignation. *She* intended to cross-question.

"If your cousin remains, Miss Eaton," Lord Taavis said more stiffly, "then you and I may as well leave, if you take my meaning."

"I take your meaning very well indeed," Alicia

told him. "And you will take mine when I assure you that I would never have set foot in this room with you if I had not thought you might reassure me about your gaming parties, the ones you are intending."

Lord Taavis glanced at Randolph, who was standing near the door, balancing himself first on one foot and then on the other in an apparent nervous condition. Then he gave his full attention to Alicia.

"You do not gamble, surely," he asked her in a teasing way. "Of course, Miss Eaton, if you do, you will be welcome here on ladies' nights. I had not thought to have them, but if I could be assured of your presence . . ."

"Either you cannot resist taunting me, sir, or you are a fool," Alicia told him. In the silence which followed, she heard Randolph sigh.

"No doubt in the country it is the fashion to berate the host," Lord Taavis sneered, "but civilized people fix limits to the extent of insult he must endure."

"I cannot insult you, sir, by simply speaking the truth," Alicia told him, ignoring the fit of coughing which Randolph had suddenly fallen into. "And, as I have just finished saying, the truth is . . ."

"No need to repeat it, Miss Eaton, I assure you," Lord Taavis said with a grimace. "Very well, then. I shall take my punishment, as long as it be brief."

Just as Alicia started to speak, there was a

sound which might have been a scream. This room was just below the part of the salon which overlooked the gardens, and remembering the three men, Alicia rose and hurried to the window.

"I would not be too curious, Miss Eaton," Lord Taavis said, hurrying to prevent her from drawing the drape. "Not all young ladies take the precautions you have taken. I will admit that it is easy for any of my guests to have found their way into the gardens, but youth is impetuous, and I fancy some young swain has found himself carried away."

"That was a scream!" Alicia told him.

"That or a faint protest," Lord Taavis drawled. "But very well. Look your fill, although no doubt they will not thank you for it. There! But we have looked too late, I fear. No doubt the lady fled back into the house, and the young gentleman was left to follow. Or perhaps they moved into the shadows, like this . . ."

Randolph's throat apparently needed clearing, for he fell into such a fit of coughing as to alert Alicia to Lord Taavis's roaming arm.

"Desist, sir," she told him. "I said I would take advantage of this opportunity to talk seriously with you, and that is what I intend."

Lord Taavis rolled his eyes up to the ceiling, but he let her have her way. Indeed, he listened closely as she told him that his invitation had caused serious problems. "Perhaps Randolph thinks I should not mention it," she said, returning to the center of the room. "If so, that is his privilege. But I find that I cannot stand by and have so much fret and fuming when it is still not very clear—at least to me—whether you intend to introduce illegal gaming or not, sir."

"Who frets and fumes about it, Miss Eaton," Lord Taavis said, eluding her question.

"My uncle does," she told him. "And with good reason. If you introduce faro or hazard or other games of that sort, he will have to take action against you. And yet you persist, sir, in behaving as though you had him in your pocket. That is the proper term, I believe. Yes, in your pocket. And you know you have not, sir. It will be a pity if you put it to the test."

"And if I *do* introduce faro, Miss Eaton," the young gentleman beside her said, "who will inform your uncle? The players will not want him to know. He has no need to be too curious about what goes on here, as long as it is discreet. I think your cousin can tell you that I am not open about my private business. He found that to be so when he tried to poke his nose in as Captain Hillary's agent."

Alicia rounded on him, her fingers clenched. "Captain Hillary is your problem, sir," she told him. "I wonder you are too blind to see it. Granted that my uncle might find it difficult if not impossible to get witnesses against you. But Captain Hillary will find a way. And then he will make a grand disclosure in his paper. And the worst result of that will be that everyone will think you were paying my uncle protection. I should not be at all surprised if it did not ruin him. I cannot let that happen to someone who has been so kind to me."

Lord Tommy Taavis did not bother to disguise his impatience. After all, he had arranged this tête-à-tête for quite another purpose than to be harangued by a beautiful young lady about what was, after all, essentially his business. Never in his entire past had he allowed himself to feel guilty for what might or might not be the fate of others, and he did not propose to feel guilty now.

"Your uncle's reputation is his own affair, Miss Eaton," he told her, stepping closer to the lamp so that the white light threw his handsome face into a ghostly outline. "You will notice, I hope, that his own son makes no such protest."

Alicia knew that the interview must soon come to an end. Had she obliged Lord Taavis, smiled and let him put his arm about her, no doubt she could have delayed this interview indefinitely, even though he was a host. Were she more artful, she might even have used her charms to lure him to make promises. As it was, simplicity and directness had not got her far.

Although Randolph said nothing, Alicia knew that what Lord Taavis had said about him must at least have stung. How destructive this man was, she marveled. He must know that Imogene was entranced by him, and yet he did nothing to discourage her. Alicia knew that if she told her cousin about this interview, Imogene would think of some way to excuse it. Doubtlessly she would tell herself that it was Lord Taavis's indirect way of getting to know her better. Alicia knew that Imogene was capable of any sort of foolishness in her present state of heart.

"You will not go back to London then?" she said, determined to make one last effort to persuade him. "Or, if you stay here, do so as a completely private person? Leave your gambling to the larger city, where no one will be hurt, no reputations ruined?"

"My dear Miss Eaton," Lord Taavis said with ill-concealed irritation, "you are persistent. Indeed, I think you are the most persistent young lady I have ever met. Let me put it this way to you. Bath appeals to something in me. It has, I think, a certain charm. And the fact that certain very wealthy gentlemen both from England and abroad are increasingly in the habit of relaxing here for weeks at a time must be taken into account. These people have a great deal of time on their hands, more than they would have in London. Their wives are following the Bath schedule, as I call it, and they must find their own entertainment. Until I came, that was very limited, I assure you."

"Thanks to my uncle!" Alicia declared defiantly.

"Thanks to the sluggishness of this little backwater," Lord Taavis told her. "Thanks to the laws against gaming passed by Parliament and the fact that such laws are taken more seriously here in the West Country. But thanks to your uncle? Oh, my dear Miss Eaton, I think you have gone too far. The gentleman may have been kind to you, but he is a quaint absurdity when it comes to upholding the law, fit for nothing more than to try a few pickpockets and bang a gavel. He is pushed about by his own wife and daughter. Why, the man is all bluff and bluster, with no will of his own. Why I should care one way or another about his future, I do not know. And now, I think, if you have asked your questions, we should . . ."

His sentence came to a premature end when His Lordship found his cravat twisted from behind in such a fashion that he turned the most peculiar shade of blue. At the same time, his feet were separated from the floor so that he dangled, much as though he were hanging from a noose.

"Randolph!" Alicia cried. "Randolph! Put him down before you throttle him!"

But Randolph did not seem to hear her. His eyes were glazed, and he twisted the cravat tighter still, making Lord Taavis's eyes bulge from their sockets.

"Mr. Bradshaw!" Alicia shouted, trusting that the gentleman who had brought her and her cousin here would still be waiting outside the door.

But Randolph flung Lord Taavis into a corner even before the smooth, gray Bradshaw burst into the room. The sounds of gagging and choking were not pleasant, but Alicia allowed Mr.

Bradshaw to attend to the victim, while she admonished Randolph.

"He had no right to speak that way of my father!" her cousin told her. "Not a word of it is true. 'Pon my soul, it was more than I could bear to hear him spoken of in that particular manner."

Alicia remembered the many times she had seen and heard Randolph treat Sir Humphrey with a marked lack of respect. Still, she supposed he felt that, although he had a right to criticize, that right belonged to no one else, with—of course—the exception of Imogene and his mother. In a word, it was a family matter.

Alicia guided Randolph toward the door, hoping they could make their escape before Lord Taavis recovered. But they were destined to be interrupted, and in the most unexpected fashion.

"Has anyone seen Imogene?" Lady Fairbreaks demanded, dashing into the room with all her feathers ruffled. "Oh dear, I can scarcely credit it, but she seems to have disappeared!"

CHAPTER TWENTY

"Someone will bear the responsibility!" Sir Humphrey declared very sternly. "This is a most disturbing situation."

In the midst of all the chaos, Alicia had had time to observe her uncle with a new respect. It had been he who had sent out for the constable with all the élan of someone who has not lost his only daughter. It was Sir Humphrey who had caused an announcement to be made to the general party that no one was to leave the building until they had been questioned. And it had been he who had decided that the investigation would begin here in Lord Taavis's elegant library. Indeed, Sir Humphrey had had no qualms in acquisitioning his host's mahogany desk, and he presently sat behind it with an air of authority which even Lady Fairbreaks seemed to find imposing. That is to say that whenever she lapsed into hysteria and Sir Humphrey commanded, she obeyed, not without the ministrations of a frightened Mrs. Tanner, who darted about the room making general use of her vinaigrette.

As for Lord Tommy Taavis, being bounced around by Randolph had left him in a sorry state. Due to a nosebleed, his cravat was not only rumpled but bloody, and his powdered hair was in disarray. The same was true of his coat of primrose satin, which sported a long rip at one shoulder. Otherwise, he was in an ugly mood and clearly kept himself under control with the greatest effort.

"I agree, it is disturbing," he told Sir Humphrey. "I simply meant to entertain friends and acquaintances, but because of your family, sir, I have been subjected to a beating and have had the added privilege of hosting a kidnapping."

The last word unfailingly threw Lady Fairbreaks into a fit of weeping, as it did now. "Silence, madam!" Sir Humphrey told her, as Mrs. Tanner plunged forward with the restorative. "Silence in this court!"

No one saw fit to remind him that, whatever else was going on, a court was not in session. Alicia thought Lord Taavis would have liked to say something of the sort, but Mr. Bradshaw tapped him on the shoulder, as a reminder of sorts, and Randolph, clearly delighted that he had some power, cleared his throat.

The story had been told so many times that Alicia did not want it to be repeated, but it seemed possible that that was precisely what Sir Humphrey wanted to do. For all his show of decisiveness, Alicia thought he might be grasping at straws.

After all, what did they really know? Mrs. Tanner had been standing beside Imogene in the salon upstairs when she saw her reading a note, of which she could see nothing except that it was, indeed, addressed to the girl in a masculine hand. As for where it had come from, she did not know, since, as she put it, "I did not want to ask, and Miss Fairbreaks did not say."

However, according to Imogene's mother, who had been the next witness, it had been an invitation from Lord Taavis to meet him in the garden in half an hour for the purpose of admiring a new sort of rose which he had had brought to Bath from France.

"I cannot think why neither Imogene nor I mentioned it to you, my dear," Lady Fairbreaks had protested when Sir Humphrey had severely accused her and her daughter of deliberately keeping him in the dark. "And I do not think it kind of you to take that attitude. Nothing could have seemed more innocently intended. You know yourself how fond Imogene is of flowers."

That had been the only moment when Alicia had been afraid that her uncle was about to fly into a fury. Otherwise he had governed himself wonderfully well, particularly when he was questioning Lord Taavis.

That gentleman, on the contrary, did not act extremely well. His ugly mood was already upon him and he declared that not only had he not sent Miss Fairbreaks a message, but that he could think of nothing more personally offensive to him than to look at roses in the moonlight with that particular young lady.

At that, Randolph had started forward, disregarding Sir Humphrey's warning call, and Lord Taavis, with Mr. Bradshaw as his advisor, was soon making a ragged sort of apology. What he meant to say, he soon explained, was that he would never have insulted Miss Fairbreaks by luring her into a situation which might very well be misunderstood by others. He then went on to offer, as further proof, that he knew nothing of flowers and had never, to his knowledge, imported anything but brandy from France.

A search having been instituted earlier, there was a pause in the proceedings for a report from the constable to the effect that they had found signs of a struggle in the garden, but nothing else. At that point Alicia had remembered the scream.

Lord Taavis protested that, although he had heard some sound or other, it was not of the sort a lady made in fright. Indeed, he spoke with so much authority on the subject that his audience concluded that he had had considerable experience in gauging those sorts of noises—as, no doubt, he had.

As for Randolph, he shrugged his shoulders. Ever since his attack on Lord Taavis, he had seemed distracted, Alicia thought. No, his attention had wandered even before that. She remembered when they had been upstairs in the grand salon and she had asked him to accompany her to the library. He had been staring out the window and . . .

"I remember something!" she declared suddenly, interrupting her uncle, who had begun a ponderous explanation of the steps he meant to have taken to assure his daughter's safe return.

"You have told us about the scream, my dear," Sir Humphrey admonished her. "And since your recollection has had no substantiation . . ."

"There were three men in the garden earlier," Alicia told him, determined that he should hear her out. "I could not see them clearly, since they were in the shadows. But one was short and one was tall and one . . ."

"What is it, my dear Alicia!" Lady Fairbreaks cried. "Why are you looking that way."

"Yes, Cousin, what is it?" Randolph demanded, looking at her sharply, as though afraid of what she was about to say. "You say one was short and one was tall . . ."

"There are a good many gentlemen in Bath to fit both categories," Lord Taavis said in a sour way. "Besides, I am quite sure that Miss Eaton is mistaken. All of my servants were busy in the house tonight, and no one else was authorized to be in the garden."

"If they were the kidnappers," Alicia told him, "I doubt whether or not they would have presented you with their credentials. There is a wall, sir, which binds your property, I would assume. And walls were built to climb over."

Lord Taavis was heard to mutter something

about sharp-tongued women, but Mr. Bradshaw whispered in his ear and he turned silent.

"The fact is," Alicia continued, "that I just remembered who they reminded me of."

"These people in the garden?" her uncle demanded. "You must be particular, you know. Witnesses can never understand the need to be particular."

"Even though you *are* here, sir, this is not a court of law," Lady Fairbreaks said in an impatient way. "If Alicia has a clue to what has happened, she must tell it in her own way."

"I do not know their names," Alicia continued, determined not to be distracted, "but I saw them just the other day in the abbey courtyard. You had stopped to talk with Mrs. Tanner, Aunt. No doubt you remember. And Imogene and I had paused a little to the side, where Lord Taavis accosted us."

"Accosted," His Lordship grumbled. "I would be pleased if you would watch your choice of words, Miss Eaton. If you mean that I engaged you in conversation, then you should say it."

In the excitement of the past half hour, some of Alicia's red curls had slipped loose from her green silk bandeau, and now she twisted one about her finger absently, her mind set on the past.

"One of the men was tall, the other short, and both walked as though they were fighters of some sort," she recollected. "And the third reminded me for all the world of a rooster. There was something about the way he strode along . . ."

She heard the muted exclamation Randolph muttered, but she did not pause. "I remember now that they stood and watched us," she went on. "Watched us most attentively. It occurred to me at the time that they might know Lord Taavis. That they were down from London . . ."

"I cannot recall anyone among my acquaintance who resembles a rooster," the viscount told her. "If you want my opinion, Sir Humphrey, your niece is clutching at straws. Why, we do not even know if your daughter has been abducted, sir. She may have had an assignation in the garden and simply wandered away."

"The message she received purported to be from you, sir!" Lady Fairbreaks cried, embarking on another fit of hysterics, bosom heaving and eyes glazed.

But Alicia scarcely noticed her aunt's condition. Randolph alone engaged her full attention, for on her description of the three men in the abbey courtyard, he had gone quite pale. All of which, in her opinion, could mean only one thing. He knew the identity of the men who had abducted Imogene. She held her breath and waited to hear what he would say.

But he said nothing. Indeed, he drew into the shadows, no doubt hoping that his agitation would not be noticed, and Alicia thought she saw him draw closer to the door.

Lady Fairbreaks was claiming attention now as

loudly as was possible for anyone with a human voice. The feathers on her turban swayed as though they were in a violent wind as she bent this way and then the other, with Mrs. Tanner dashing about her in a frantic manner. Lord Taavis remained stoic in the face of her distress, just as did Mr. Bradshaw, who stood beside him. But Sir Humphrey could not endure the racket. At least that was what he bellowed over and over again.

In the midst of this distraction, Randolph managed to slip out the door with Alicia behind him, holding up the skirts of her polonaise gown with both hands, quite determined not to let him go until he had told her what he knew about the three men she had described.

It happened that young Soupcon, who was waiting in the hall outside along with scores of the invited guests, allowed Randolph to pass. But Alicia was another matter.

"Tell me what is going on in the library, Miss Eaton!" he demanded, stepping in her path. "Has there been news of Imogene? I mean to say, Miss Fairbreaks, is she safe? 'Pon my word, I *must* know!"

Alicia actually pushed him aside and made her way toward the stairs which led up to the grand salon, the stairs which Randolph was, even now, in the process of negotiating.

"If you want to follow your cousin, there is a better way," she heard someone say. Turning, she found Captain Hillary beside her at the bottom of the stairs.

"What are you saying?" Alicia demanded in an agitated way. "In a moment I will have lost him."

"There is only one way out of the front of the house," the captain told her, his dark eyes intent on hers. "Your cousin will doubtless be able to persuade the constable or one of his deputies to let him leave, once he has proved himself to be the brother of the missing person. But the proving will take time. I can show you a way out of this house which will allow us to be waiting on the Royal Crescent when your cousin starts on his way to wherever he is going in such a hurry."

"Then show me," Alicia said with sudden determination. "I realize that you only want a story, but just now that does not matter to me. I am convinced that Randolph knows who has taken Imogene, and that if we follow him, we will find out where she is right now."

CHAPTER TWENTY-ONE

Following Randolph did not turn out to be a simple task, however. First of all, contrary to Captain Hillary's expectations, Alicia's cousin either could not talk his way out of the house or else he did not try, a fact which created no little confusion, since the captain and Alicia watched the front door for quite ten minutes before he made an appearance, and then not out the door but rather dropping from a window, which was fortunately within their view.

Captain Hillary had been as good as his word when it had come to their ease in leaving the house by the back way. When Alicia had asked him how he knew that a certain door opened into a small back hall which, in turn, led directly to the garden, he had murmured something about having been brought up in a house like this. It came to Alicia at that moment, as they lingered in the shadows until he could ascertain if anyone was watching, that she knew very little about his past, except that he had been with the army in America during the revolution. And then she asked herself why she *should* know anything at all. Certainly she was not curious! After all, the only reason she was with him now was because she must do something to rescue Imogene.

"The only way we can get to the front of the house is to go over the wall at the back," the captain murmured, which was, Alicia thought, an unnecessary comment, since all the houses in the Royal Crescent were joined to one another. "There is a deputy stalking about over there, but I think if we could manage just here . . ."

Taking her by the hand, the captain had hurried to a section of the wall which was lower than the rest, and fortunately in an even deeper shadow than the one they had stood in before, thanks to a hovering beech tree. Before she knew what he was about, he had taken her by her slim waist and set her, muslin and satin flying, on the top of the wall; whereupon he swung himself up beside her, leaped to the ground on the other side, and directly she was being lowered in his arms.

Alicia could not ignore the fact that the touch of his hands sent her into a quiver. But she was determined that her attitude toward him should not appear to change.

"I cannot think why you should have wanted to take me with you, sir," she said, adjusting her gown. "Clearly I am nothing but a liability."

"You know your cousins," Captain Hillary replied, taking her hand again and leading her down the narrow lane which backed the Crescent. "This is an uncertain situation, and no one should know how to deal with them better than you. After all, for some reason or other you struck on the idea that Randolph is going to the place his sister has been taken, which we can only hope is true."

Alicia discovered that she was being hurried along too rapidly to allow for rational thought. It was certainly an extraordinary thing that, without a word of explanation as to why she had wanted to follow Randolph, Captain Hillary had offered to help her. And when the explanation had come, he had not made delays by asking why it was she thought so. What a poor job she would have made of that, she thought now, for it had only been the look on Randolph's face when she had described the three men in the garden which had alerted her.

They had rounded the end of the Crescent now, and Alicia was quite breathless. Indeed, she was grateful when the captain suggested they simply cross the street, which was lined with carriages, and wait for Randolph to emerge. It would be easy enough not to be noticed, in his opinion, since there was a cluster of postilions who had deserted their master's curricles, barouches, and phaetons in order to hang about the doorway of Lord Taavis's establishment, the arrival of the constable and his deputies having, no doubt, alerted them to the fact that all was not well inside. Indeed, a closer look established the fact that they were being questioned by an earnest gentleman with a very red face and a puzzled expression.

"I'll lay odds that the kidnappers managed to get your cousin away without being seen," Captain Hillary said in a low voice, taking Alicia's arm in order to guide her past the various equipages to a point where they were directly between the town below and the house.

"Isn't it possible that Randolph is already gone?" Alicia demanded. "If I have lost him . . ."

"I know. I know," the captain told her. "It will all be my fault. But remember that he chose to make his way out of the house through the salon upstairs, and you will recall that that was crowded. Furthermore, there is the matter of persuading whoever was put to guard the door that, as Sir Humphrey's son, he should have the right to leave the house. It is just possible that is what is delaying him right now. But as for having already left . . ."

At that particular moment a distraction occurred which sent the knot of postilions about the door, together with the red-faced gentleman, flying down the street in the other direction.

"One of the horses has tried to bolt for it," Captain Hillary told Alicia. "What a moment this would be for Randolph to make his escape."

As though that were a cue, a window on the ground floor opened, and a figure slipped out and onto the ground.

"And there he is!" Alicia heard Captain Hillary

whisper triumphantly. "Come along, Miss Eaton, and we will see how much he knows about what has happened to his sister."

Alicia had expected Randolph to hurry along the curve of the Crescent, following the curve of the white columned, terraced houses. But, instead, behaving in the most extraordinary way, he cowered in doorways and on area steps, as though someone was pursuing him. Three leaps ahead, a quick glance backward, and another crouch was as good a way as another to describe his general progress, while Alicia and Captain Hillary followed at a leisurely pace from behind the protection of the carriages which lined the Crescent on the other side.

"I think your cousin has a flair for the dramatic," Captain Hillary murmured. "Never mind. Let him indulge himself in his playacting as long as he leads us to his sister."

Randolph had now reached Brock Street, where a row of houses opened the way out into the Circus, where still another group of terraced houses sat overlooking the town. In and out of shadows Randolph dodged, his head always turned back over his shoulder, so that Alicia thought it was a miracle that he did not run straight into something. Once, in fact, he did trip over his own feet and fall, and the two across the street from him could hear him swearing in the awful sort of way people will do when they think they are alone.

"All this has something to do with the three

men I saw in the garden," Alicia murmured when her cousin had once again disappeared down a flight of area stairs. "When I described them, I could tell at once he knew who they were. And if they had not had something to do with Imogene's disappearance, I do not think he would be behaving in this extraordinary way."

Captain Hillary's arm tightened on hers as Randolph appeared again, a fleeing shadow, only to halt and hide like a hunted animal on the darkened steps of another porch.

"If he recognized the men whom you described," the captain said in a very low voice indeed, "then why do you suppose he did not simply tell your father their names? Either they were guests . . ."

"If their clothing was any indication," Alicia told him, "they were definitely not guests."

"All right then. Let us say that unless they were servants they had no right on Lord Taavis's grounds. It would seem logical to assume, since your cousin was lured to the garden, that she was abducted there by them."

Randolph had sprinted ahead across the Circus toward Gay Street, and the two were forced to hold their speculations in abeyance while they hurried after him. Once on the slope of Gay Street, Randolph returned to his former halting progress, and it was then, as they waited in the shadows just across the street, that Alicia was suddenly quite certain that she had had an insight.

"I think they must have been members of the Rimrod Ring," she whispered to the captain, leaning so close to him that she knew he must feel her breath on his cheek. She hoped he would not misinterpret this intimacy. It was only because it was necessary, given the circumstances, that they should stand so close together and that he should always be holding her, either by the arm or hand. When this was over at last, they could go back to crossing swords with one another. But for the moment they needed one another's help.

"You may be right," Captain Hillary said in a low voice. A lighted candle had been set in the window of a house they were just passing, and for a moment she saw something of his face. What had she been expecting, she wondered? That he would still be mocking her for her ideas? And yet she was certain that there had been something quite different from mockery in his expression as he looked down at her.

"After all, Randolph fancies himself a member," Alicia said with a growing sense of horror. "I am not certain that he knows any other criminals except for Lord Taavis, and that is not quite the same."

Randolph ran ahead again, a swift-moving shadow on the other side of the street. They followed, pausing as he paused.

"Oh, that would be quite terrible!" Alicia whispered. "I mean if it is true that there are scores of members and all of them hardened criminals down from London, what will have happened to

Imogene already! Oh, it is all Randolph's fault! No doubt they took her because they knew that, through him, they could force his father to pay a big ransom. An important gang like that would not hesitate to do anything. They have seen Randolph is a fool and . . ."

"Do not upset yourself," her companion murmured, and she felt him press one of her hands between both of his. It was a strangely comforting gesture. "The truth is that after I talked with you the other day, I made inquiries of people who would know something about any gang either here or in London if there were anything to know. And no one has ever heard of the Rimrod Ring."

"How strange," Alicia whispered. "Do you suppose Randolph could have made it up? Why would he do such a thing?"

"You said he told it to his friend Soupcon while he was in his cups," he murmured, and now she could almost feel the touch of his lips, he was so close. "Perhaps it was his way of boasting. Because the only person I could find who had ever even heard the name Rimrod was an old fellow who said he knew a Frank Rimrod when he was at Newgate but that it was impossible that he could have a gang, since he was the sort of fellow who makes a hash out of everything he touches."

Feeling more bewildered than ever, Alicia let him lead her on until Randolph finally paused in front of a rather shabby house on a street which turned off Gay. As he raised his hand to knock,

Captain Hillary broke the quiet of the night with a greeting.

"Hello, my dear fellow," he said, as he and Alicia crossed the cobbled street together. "Yes, go ahead and knock. Is it too much for us to hope that you have led us to your sister?"

CHAPTER TWENTY-TWO

Abduction, as the Rimrod Ring discovered to their dismay, was not a simple crime. Unlike snatching and grabbing, in which case the coins or other valuables gave no trouble, kidnapping, by its own definition, requires that you deal with a human being, who is not likely to be as docile as a few guineas or a pocket watch.

The first part had been easy. Frank Rimrod, always a careful observer, had noted the way Miss Fairbreaks had flirted with Lord Taavis that morning in the abbey square, and it had been his notion that she be sent a note, once the party had started, inviting her to meet His Lordship in the garden. Granted that how the note should get from his hands to hers had caused a little trouble, but operating under the conviction that the simple ways are always the best, Frank had sent Jack Farmer out to give the message, neatly folded, to the first passing urchin who wanted to earn a shilling.

After that everything went on apace. The urchin strolled up Gay Street, full of whistles and general high spirits to have so much money in his pocket, and the three members of the Rimrod Ring followed behind. Pausing across the street from Lord Taavis's house on the Royal Crescent, they watched the note conveyed into a footman's hand. Then it was off and around to the back of the row of houses and over the wall into the garden. All "sound as a roast" as Tom Whitley would say.

The trouble started when Imogene fell into their trap. In the first place, it had been no easy matter to subdue her. When Frank had grabbed her from behind, she had apparently jumped to quite the wrong conclusion as to his identity, which given the situation, was perhaps only natural. At all events he was rewarded with a sound kiss on the cheek and might have suffered still other endearments had Imogene not realized that he was a far cry from the gentleman she had expected to see.

Then the screaming had begun. Fortunately Jack Farmer had a neckerchief which he stuffed into Imogene's obliging mouth. But all three of them had been adither, even though Frank had not let it show, as to whether anyone had heard her. As a consequence, there had been a brief pause in the shadows, which Jack Farmer called "hiding low," and then they were up and over the wall again, with the victim putting up such a struggle that Tom Whitley had proposed a slight crack on the head.

"It's not that I'm a great one for violence," he

said as Imogene jumped on his toes, "but this one is slippery as a fish, and I don't mind saying so."

At precisely that point Frank Rimrod realized that the project was destined not to go as well as he had hoped.

"The blindfold!" he told his companion. "I'll be a sapskull if we didn't forget that part of it!"

Imogene, who was tossing herself about in Jack Farmer's arms, made a lengthy comment which, thanks to the neckerchief in her mouth, was unintelligible but sounded, nonetheless, in the nature of a threat. This protest came to a sudden end, however, when Tom Whitley expressed his sincere hope that the oversight on their part would not require that she be put in a bag and thrown into the river. Indeed, at this point Imogene fell into a swoon which was so deep that, although they had come with ropes, there was no necessity to tie her.

Transportation was provided in the form of a shabby sedan chair which Jack Farmer had "borrowed" the night before from the area down near the Pump Room, where such forms of transportation were stored. Jack Farmer took the front poles and Tom Whitley the back, and Frank walked along the side with one eye to the window to make certain that Miss Fairbreaks remained in her unconscious state. As for the matter of their subsequent identification once she was released, he put it out of his mind. What was important now was to wait and see what response Sir Humphrey would make once he returned home and found the ransom message which Jack Farmer had pushed under the magistrate's door earlier in the evening.

There was, thankfully, no sign of Mrs. Simpson when they reached the lodging house, and Frank was able to let them in with his key with no interference. As for Imogene, she had recovered from her swoon sufficiently to be strictly restrained by Tom Whitley, who carried her up the stairs. By the time they had reached the Rimrod Ring's apartment, with the door shut behind, the girl had managed to remove the neckerchief used as a gag and had begun to express herself in a lusty manner. Furthermore, when Jack Farmer put his hand over her mouth, she bit him with so much relish that tears came into his eyes.

After that, the problem was to overcome her, since having tasted victory, she became a whirlwind, racing around the room in a twirl of lilac satin and white lace, and striking out at anyone who approached her with anything she could lay her hands on, all of which included several pieces of Mrs. Simpson's china that she used to decorate the rooms, not to mention a wall mirror of which the landlady was very fond. In the midst of all this activity, it came as a distinct shock to the three members of the Rimrod Ring to hear a knock sound on the door.

Considering the noise they had been making, it was useless to pretend that they were not at home. Indeed, Mrs. Simpson did not give them any time to indulge in a little pretense, for with her latchkey, she opened the door and looked around the room with a distinct expression of dismay in her narrow eyes.

Before the landlady could make any comment on the situation, Imogene cast herself into the other woman's arms. "Save me!" she cried. "Protect me!" And then she added other utterances of an appropriate nature from one who has recently been abducted.

Mrs. Simpson calmed the girl in a time-honored way, telling her that everything was certain to be all right now and that she would protect her.

"As for these gentlemen," the landlady said severely, "it is clear that they have been ill-advised. Either that or it has all been a prank."

She said that last in such a suggestive way as to cause Frank Rimrod to leap to attention.

"A prank!" he cried. "Of course, that was precisely what it was. Tell me, Miss Fairbreaks, would anyone in their right mind choose to kidnap the daughter of the town's leading magistrate? Why, the risk is too considerable!"

In the midst of these disclaimers, a knock was heard on the door downstairs. It was dusk now, and Mrs. Simpson lighted a candle before she went down the narrow stairs, telling Imogene to stay exactly where she was, and as a parting shot over her thin shoulder, advising the three disheartened abductors to allow her to take charge.

There followed the sound of voices, and footsteps on the stairs. First Randolph slunk into the room. Then Captain Hillary appeared in the low-ceilinged chamber with Miss Alicia Eaton at his side.

The joy with which Imogene received them can, no doubt, be imagined. Safe in Alicia's arms, she glared at Mr. Rimrod, who had collapsed disconsolately onto a chair and was staring at what remained of a fire in the hearth. Deprived of the leadership they needed, Tom Whitley and Jack Farmer were applying themselves to the wounds Imogene had brought on them, the former seeing to the bandaging of a big toe, while the latter applied raw gin to a variety of cuts and bruises before taking an internal dose.

"Well," Captain Hillary declared, "this is a pretty situation which, I think, demands an explanation."

"Why, as for that, sir," Mrs. Simpson said, "I can vouch for these three gentlemen. I believe this was nothing but a prank. Thoughtless, no doubt, and disturbing to the lady. But then brothers are rarely as careful as they should be of their sister's feelings."

"Brothers!" Imogene demanded. "What has Randolph to do with this, pray?"

Mrs. Simpson pretended to a mild confusion, while Frank Rimrod, always alert to a change in the situation, raised his head.

"I only thought that since he so often visited these gentlemen, he might have played some part in this escapade," she told them.

"You visited these people, Randolph?" Imogene demanded.

"That explains how he knew where to come this evening," Captain Hillary murmured to Alicia.

"You had no right to follow me!" Randolph retorted angrily. "I guessed these fellows had her because I saw them earlier in the garden. If you and my cousin had not interfered, sir, this matter would have been well settled now."

Somewhere in the excitement of the evening, Alicia had lost her green silk bandeau, and it was necessary to sweep her curls back from her face.

"I think you owe us an explanation, Randolph," she said firmly. "What have you to do with these—these gentlemen?"

Randolph had the good grace to look disconcerted. "I was using them to get information about the underworld in Bath," he mumbled. "'Pon my soul, Alicia, what an embarrassing question to ask. The captain knows! After all, I was doing it for him and for his paper."

It was dusk now, and the single candle Mrs. Simpson had lighted cast shadows all about the room, causing Captain Hillary's face to seem even darker. Alicia could tell little of what he was thinking by looking at him, and she felt a sudden chill. There had been companionship when they had hurried down Gay Street together, following her cousin. And the excitement of finding Imogene which had followed had made her feel quite close to him. Now, however, she recalled the times she had begged him not to let Randolph get involved. Well, this had been the result of his failure to take her seriously. She supposed she should feel some satisfaction, but she did not.

"What was the last request I made of you, sir?" the captain asked her cousin with a curt nod in his direction. "Was it not to desist in your investigation? It was brought to my notice"—and here he glanced at Alicia—"that you had encountered certain difficulties which might put your safety in question. I told you, you will remember . . ."

"I had a right to make investigations on my own," Randolph said defiantly. "You could not prevent me from doing that."

Frank Rimrod had been listening to all this with considerable attention, and even Tom Whitley and Jack Farmer seemed to find it mildly diverting, although their major concern was for the passing of the bottle between them at regular intervals.

"I'll be a gudgeon if there hasn't been a misunderstanding," Frank Rimrod declared, springing to his feet with the first show of animation he had demonstrated since his attempt to commit a major crime had come to such an ignominious conclusion. "Mr. Fairbreaks here has been accepting protection money. Not only from my gang, mind, but from all sorts of other people. We pay in return for immunity as far as the law's concerned in this city. The money goes straight from his hands to his father's."

Captain Hillary stiffened. "Is this the truth?" he questioned Randolph.

Alicia could not help but feel sorry for her cousin. It was clear that he was in such a state of confusion that he could not find his place. Out of the stammerings and stutters which followed, she concluded that he had somehow believed he was being hired by the Rimrod Ring and others."

"Hired!" Frank Rimrod shouted. "Why, I ask you, how could he ever have been hired, when he was never asked to do a thing? Except provide protection through his father. That was the only use he was to us!"

Mrs. Simpson, in her even-mannered way, ventured that she thought there had been a clear misunderstanding. She, at least, was willing to believe that Randolph had never thought he was accepting protection money. Just so, Frank Rimrod had never realized that Randolph had thought he was being paid for being a part of the Rimrod Ring and others. All of which got Randolph started, and he went on and on about how everything had been confused. He had wanted to be part of the underground, he told them, in order to gather information.

Now that Alicia knew for certain that Captain Hillary had acted on what she had told him and, indeed, had discouraged her cousin from such escapades, she tried to catch his eye to let him know that she completely understood and held no grudge against him. But now he seemed to look everywhere in the room except at her.

"Do you mean to bring charges, Miss Fairbreaks?" he asked Imogene.

"It's me who should claim damages," Tom Whitley grumbled, apparently in reference to his big toe which Imogene had stepped on.

"We only meant to make our reputation, miss," Jack Farmer told Imogene. "We never meant to hurt you or to cause an upset like."

Alicia wondered how he had thought he could avoid upset in a kidnapping attempt, but another look at his vacant expression assured her that Mr. Farmer had not thought the matter out in detail, to put the kindest light on it.

"I daresay that if the lady prosecutes, the bit about her brother will come out," Mrs. Simpson suggested shrewdly. "Had you considered that, Mr. Rimrod?"

The suggestion was enough to make Frank prick up his ears. Indeed, he quite recovered his self-possession at the thought of attempted blackmail. There would, of course, be that consideration, he replied. And then, of course, the other people who had been paying Randolph what they thought was protection would be put into a state of irritation to discover that their money had bought them nothing and that it had only been good fortune which had kept them from being hauled before Sir Humphrey. They would be apt to cause a problem, Frank Rimrod mentioned. Young Mr. Fairbreaks might find himself in a gutter some fine night with his throat cut from ear to ear.

At this Imogene screamed and told her brother that no one must ever know what had happened here. "If I say nothing about being kidnapped," she said, "and Mr. Rimrod says nothing about the trouble Randolph has got himself into, and if Captain Hillary . . ."

The eyes of everyone in the room turned to the captain. Had he, Alicia wondered, deliberately moved so that his face was in the shadows? Would he insist on reporting all this, as was his right? Indeed, was it not his duty to do so?

"I do not think we can ask him to be silent," she said in a low voice. "Captain Hillary has made no secret from the start that he intends to eliminate the criminal element in Bath. Why, thanks to him, my uncle has made renewed efforts to administer justice. If it ever should come out that what has happened here tonight and in the days before had been covered up, where would his credibility be? We cannot ask that much of him, I think."

Frank Rimrod declared that he could find it in himself to ask that and a good deal more. In this Imogene and her brother quite concurred, so that together with Mrs. Simpson, Tom Whitley, and Jack Farmer they presented a united front.

But, as it happened, there was no need for argument. In a low voice Captain Hillary declared that he had no intention of playing into Lord Tommy Taavis's hand.

"You were quite right, Miss Eaton, when you suggested that afternoon at your aunt's entertainment that Lord Taavis would do anything he could to put your uncle at fault."

Remembering how outspoken she had been on that occasion, Alicia flushed.

"Everyone should have taken you more seriously than they did, including me," Captain Hillary went on slowly. "Now Lord Taavis has managed to play host to Sir Humphrey, which will mean tongues will wag. Worse, if this business about his son and daughter comes out, his name will be further tarnished, and people being what they are, his reputation, too, no matter how unfairly. And who will stand to gain? Only Lord Taavis. No doubt he will feel free to play at gaming any way he likes."

Tom Whitley stated his firm conviction that the gentleman was right, and Jack Farmer proposed a toast, all of which resulted in Frank Rimrod telling them in no uncertain terms to be quiet.

"Do you mean to write nothing about Randolph's association with these people?" Alicia asked. "Have you decided not to expose the circumstances of Imogene's abduction?"

Despite the shadows, she saw the captain smile. "As for Randolph," he continued, "he was clearly the victim of a strange misunderstanding. And Miss Fairbreaks's abduction was so inept that one can scarcely call it a crime."

"Her father may not think so, sir," Mrs. Simpson told him, clearly puzzled about the course events were taking.

"I do not want any scandal," Imogene told

them. "If all the circumstances were known, I would be a laughingstock."

"And my reputation would be even worse than it already is," Randolph told them in a doleful voice.

"I will need the cooperation of Mr. Rimrod," Captain Hillary proposed, at which that gentleman declared he was willing to make any sort of bargain.

"In the first place," the captain told him, "you must assure me that you and your companions will give up your criminal ambitions. At least as long as you are in Bath."

"Damme if we won't, sir," Frank Rimrod told him fervently, to a backdrop of mumbled comments from Tom Whitley and Jack Farmer which seemed to indicate agreement.

"Furthermore," Captain Hillary continued, "you must give me what information you have about underworld activities in this city. The names and occupations of those people who made Randolph such generous offers should suffice."

"No sooner said than done, sir!" the leader of the Rimrod Ring replied. "I'd put it down in writing if someone will help me with the words."

"All that can be accomplished in my office," the captain told him, "after we have seen Randolph and his sister and Miss Eaton home. A message can be sent to the Royal Crescent to the effect that Miss Fairbreaks is safe."

"But what will I tell them?" Imogene demanded.

"I think you should say that when you discovered that the message inviting you into the garden was a ruse, you were angry and went home in a temper," Alicia said.

"And how will we account for our disappearance?" Randolph demanded.

"We can say we guessed what might have happened and went off to find your sister," Alicia told him, warming to the task of subterfuge.

"All of which," the captain noted, "is more or less the truth."

Mrs. Simpson applauded the suggestion and was in the process of announcing that her lips were sealed, when a noise outside one of the windows attracted her attention.

"Robbers!" she cried, the responsibilities of her occupation coming to the fore. "Thieves! Someone is climbing up the trellis! I can hear the cracking of the branches. Call the watchman! Sound the alarm!"

Eager to avoid this possibility, Frank Rimrod and his companions hurried to the window and raised it in a second, whereupon young Soupcon came tumbling into the room.

"Miss Fairbreaks!" he shouted, lying supine on the floor. "Imogene! I have come to the rescue! Never fear!"

The candlelight was not so faint that Alicia could not see her cousin color prettily. Indeed, she clapped her hands in delight.

It took a while, however, to convince young Soupcon that matters had already been sorted out. Dusting himself off, he told them that, having followed the captain and Miss Eaton from the Royal Crescent and finding the door of the boardinghouse locked after they had entered, he had come to the conclusion that they had been taken captives, as well. Three times the trellis had repelled him. Three times he had picked himself up from the ground and tried again. Quite overcome with emotion, Imogene went to him and took his hand. An explanation followed, and had the company not been quite so thick around them, Alicia thought there might have been an embrace, as well.

"Tomorrow, Miss Eaton," Captain Hillary said in a low voice as they were leaving, "the editorial will be written. I wonder if you would like to give your opinion on it before I see it printed?"

Alicia thought he could have said nothing at this moment more calculated to give her pleasure.

"You take me seriously at last, sir," she murmured.

The captain's dark eyes met hers and lingered.

"More seriously than you imagine, Miss Eaton," he told her. "If you will give me the opportunity, I swear I will prove that to you and more."

CHAPTER TWENTY-THREE

This time it was Sir Humphrey who decided on the celebration. Quite to Lady Fairbreaks's amazement, he not only named the night but arranged to have musicians playing at a certain spot which he reserved in the middle of Spring Gardens on the other side of the river. And since it was a charming evening, with the moon as silver as the sun is sometimes gold, a delightful time was had by all.

"My uncle actually said that no expense would be too great," Alicia told Captain Hillary as they promenaded under a sky shot full of stars. "It put my aunt in such a flurry that for the past week there has been no peace about the house."

She did not add that whatever confusion there had been was such a happy change from all the scolds and bothers of the past that it had been more than welcome. Time enough later on to make such confidences. At present the captain showed much more interest in Alicia's parents, and indeed had mentioned that he was looking forward to meeting them.

All that, however, was in the future. Just now she meant to live for tonight. The fireflies were everywhere, darting spots of light which echoed the glow of the flickering candles. Tables groaned with jellies and creams and pickled salmon and every sort of cold collation, and there was a deal of laughter everywhere.

What a happy sight it was, Alicia thought, as she and the captain paused to survey the company. The editorial which he had written had sent scores of dubious-looking ladies and gentlemen of low degree scurrying out of the city, together with the more aristocratic company of Lord Tommy Taavis, who, having read the writing on the wall as well as on the pages of *The Gazette*, had decided that London was more to his liking than Bath. As for the Rimrod Ring, they were now dedicated to the cause of justice, and it was said that Frank Rimrod had become Sir Humphrey's right-hand man. Indeed, he and his two companions were part of the company tonight, with Mrs. Simpson leaning on Frank Rimrod's arm.

As for Imogene, she seemed to be everywhere at once, with young Soupcon beside her, both of them beaming so cheerfully that Alicia was certain that an announcement would be soon in coming. Randolph, deprived of the company of Soupcon for the moment, was consoling himself with a very pretty lady who seemed to find him endlessly amusing, if her peals of laughter were any indication.

But it was Sir Humphrey and Lady Fairbreaks

who seemed most contented in one another's company. Alicia's uncle was dressed in what was for him the height of fashion—a pink satin coat and an embroidered waistcoat, which only seemed a size or two too large. Wandering along the gravel paths, he dispensed greetings to his guests with an enthusiasm he usually reserved for condemning prisoners at the bar, while Lady Fairbreaks nodded her ostrich feathers in all directions and beamed with a benevolence rarely displayed in her husband's company.

Even Mrs. Tanner seemed transformed, appearing on the arm of Mr. Tanner, who had apparently abandoned his misanthropy for the evening.

"This could pass for a happy ending," Alicia observed as she and the captain turned and strolled down to the river. "And to think it all began so badly."

"Do you remember that morning in the Pump Room when you sat down at my table?" Captain Hillary asked her.

"How unscrupulous I thought you were!"

"And the visit you made me at my office?"

Someday, Alicia thought, as she nodded, she would tell about the moment when she had come to love him, with the sunlight spraying through the window and the presses pounding and the sudden sense of closeness. Even though she had not thought he believed her, even though she had left him in a rage. . . .

But there was no need to remember, at least

not now, with the moon shining on the water and Bath waiting for them across the river. Imogene would have her wish, no doubt, and live on the Royal Crescent, but Alicia thought with fondness of a smaller building, just off York Street, with the smell of printer's ink in the air and cozy rooms for living overhead.

No, there was no need to remember when so much could happen now. She turned her head to look at him, and not knowing how it happened, found herself in his embrace. And quite suddenly the happy ending became a new beginning, with the future shining just as brightly as the moon shone on the river at their feet.

THE WILD ONE

by
MARIANNE HARVEY
bestselling author of *The Dark Horseman*
and *The Proud Hunter*

Proud, beautiful Judith—raised by her stern
grandmother on the savage Cornish coast—
boldly abandoned herself to one man and sought
solace in the arms of another. But only one man
could tame her, could match her fiery spirit,
could fulfill the passionate promise of rapturous,
timeless love.

A Dell Book $2.95   (19207-2)

THE TAMING

Aleen Malcolm

Cameron—daring, impetuous girl/woman who has never known a life beyond the windswept wilds of the Scottish countryside.

Alex Sinclair—high-born and quick-tempered, finds more than passion in the heart of his headstrong ward Cameron.

Torn between her passion for freedom and her long-denied love for Alex, Cameron is thrust into the dazzling social whirl of 18th century Edinburgh and comes to know the fulfillment of deep and dauntless love.

A Dell Book $3.25

Dell Bestsellers